Silenced at the Summer Social

With warm wishes

Elizabeth Ducie

A Chudleigh Phoenix Publications Book

Copyright © 2024 Elizabeth Ducie

Cover design: Berni Stevens

Internal illustration: Otis Lea-Weston

The right of Elizabeth Ducie to be identified as the Author of the Work has been asserted by her in accordance with the Copyright, Designs and Patents Act 1988.

All rights reserved. No part of this publication may be reproduced, stored in a retrieval system or transmitted in any form or by any means without the prior consent of the author, nor be otherwise circulated in any form of binding or cover other than that in which it is published and without a similar condition, including this condition, being imposed on the subsequent purchaser.

ISBN (paperback): 978-1-913020-23-1

ISBN (ebook): 978-1-913020-24-8

Chudleigh Phoenix Publications

For the people of Chudleigh who welcomed two townies
with open arms and turned them into country folk

Summer Social in the grounds of Mountjoy Manor

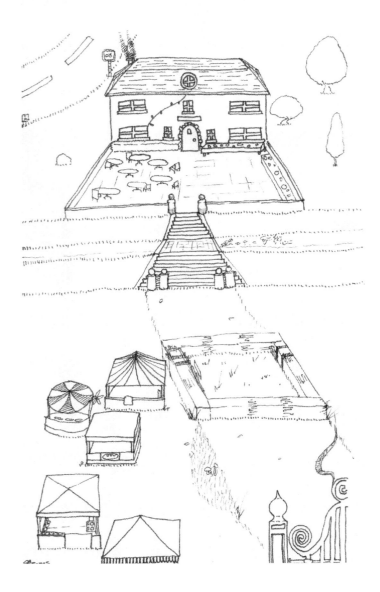

PROLOGUE
SUNDAY 1ˢᵀ SEPTEMBER 2024

Rohan Banerjee had never seen Esther Steele looking so relaxed – or so beautiful.

"I do think it's kind of Olga to open her grounds for the village in this way, don't you, Rohan?"

She looked cool in a pale green and pink floral dress, huge shades, and a floppy straw hat from which her almost white-blonde hair streamed down her back. He grinned at her as she tugged at his hand, trying to pull him up the lane even faster, like an excited child. Anyone would think she'd never been to a village fete before. But then he remembered. Esther had suffered from anxiety attacks since a child and had only just recently started going out and about again. So maybe this was a real treat for her.

"Yes, it's a big ask, letting a bunch of strangers traipse all over the lawns. But I reckon she loves the chance to play lady of the manor now and again." Rohan let go of Esther's hand to pull some change from his pocket. "How much do you want, Roger? I heard you volunteered to run the ticket booth."

A middle-aged man with a black pencil moustache was seated under a huge sunshade. "Volunteered? Volun-told more like. But you know what my Celia's like when she gets involved in a project. And put her together with Olga and she's even worse." He paused and pointed to a sign on the front of the table. "£1 each to enter, to include a tea or coffee and a copy of the programme."

"Well at least you're able to sit down, Roger," Esther said. "I understand Celia's running the tea tent. She's not going to get much time to sit down, now is she?"

"Very true, Esther. Very true. Have a good afternoon – and don't forget to spend lots of money. It's all in a good cause." Roger waved to the pair before turning to a family that had just appeared through the gates and was waiting to pay their entrance fee.

"What do you want to do first?" Rohan asked as the pair strolled around the side of Mountjoy Manor and out onto the back lawn. He read from the programme. "There's live music at the top of the hour. And then the dog show starts after that. Plus we've got all the stalls to look at."

They stopped in amazement at the scene in front of them. The gardens had been transformed. The terrace outside the huge kitchen was covered with a giant gazebo full of tables and chairs. Celia Richardson was standing behind a trestle at one end filling cups from an urn. A second trestle was piled high with cakes and biscuits.

At the bottom of the slope, on the flattest part of the grounds, an arena had been set up, surrounded by straw bales that would act both as a border for the performance area and seating for the audience. Every other corner was full of stalls, some covered, some open to the thankfully dry and warm weather.

"Let's stroll around and see where everything is to start with," Esther said, "then grab a table near the edge of the terrace. We'll be able to hear the singing from there and have coffee and a cake at the same time."

The day was a huge success. All the stalls did well. In fact several sold out. The tea tent certainly proved very popular. And the dog show brought folks in from as far away as

Newton Abbot, Ashburton and Exeter.

Everyone agreed the hog roast was a perfect way to end the event and the fireworks were let off as soon as it was dark, so even the young children were able to stay up and watch. But by the time the last visitors disappeared, and the doors closed at ten, the organisers had been on their feet for fourteen hours or more. Rohan and Esther hadn't had anything to do all afternoon but volunteered to help shut things down at the end of the event.

Olga Mountjoy gathered everyone together on the terrace. "Okay, folks, I don't know about you, but I'm bushed. So I'm going to suggest we leave everything exactly as it is." She held up a hand as Celia opened her mouth to argue. "No, honey, I know you don't want to leave me with a mess, but trust me, I'm not going to hang around for one more minute. Go home, all of you. We'll reassemble at nine tomorrow and clear up. Then I'll provide brunch for all the helpers. How does that sound?"

There were nods of agreement and everyone started to move towards the exit when a long scream ripped through the darkness. It came from the swimming pool room, situated below the terrace and opening onto the garden. Everyone turned and rushed down the slope, Rohan leading the way. He stopped abruptly when he arrived at the doorway and saw the scene before him.

Penny Conway was standing at the side of the pool, pointing with a trembling finger at the body floating face down in the water.

It was a woman, fully-clothed in an old-fashioned skirt and jacket, red and black check and far too heavy-looking for the time of year. But it was an outfit everyone would recognise. Rohan knew he was telling nobody anything they didn't know when he said, "It's Josephine Hillson."

He did not need to say, either, that the woman was very obviously dead.

CHAPTER 1
SATURDAY 24ᵀᴴ AUGUST
(EIGHT DAYS EARLIER)

"There you go, Miss Hillson. A cappuccino and one of my special chocolate chip cookies. Just as you ordered."

"Thank you, Celia." The stout upright woman in the thick check suit took a sip from the cup and then dabbed her mouth with the dainty lace handkerchief she pulled out of her sleeve. She gave a contented sigh and leaned back in her chair. "I do so look forward to my little treat every Saturday morning."

"And why not? You've worked hard all your life. It's time you took it a bit easy and enjoyed yourself." Celia Richardson wiped down the counter, even though she'd done it just moments before and knew there were no crumbs to get rid of.

It was late morning and the lull between the early morning orders from people waiting for the bus into Exeter for a day's shopping, and the inevitable lunchtime rush. Apart from Roger, who was serving a mother and teenage twins in the grocery area, Celia and Miss Hillson were alone in Cosy Café.

Celia knew her customer's first name was Josephine, but

she would never call her that. She was Miss Hillson when Celia and Roger were in her class in the primary school forty years ago, and she was still Miss Hillson today. And many other people in the village treated the elderly woman with the same level of respect. Now, Celia picked up her own coffee and leaned on the counter, ready for a little gossip. "Even though you're retired, you're still pretty busy, aren't you?"

Josephine Hillson nodded. "I have to admit, the Parish Council keeps me out of mischief. The main meeting's only once a month, but when you add in all the extra sub-committees, dealing with finance, planning and the like, we have meetings most weeks. And I make it my practice to get the minutes typed up and sent out every Saturday morning before I come in here. That way, I can start each week with a clear conscience, knowing there's nothing hanging over me to be carried forward."

Miss Hillson took a nibble of her biscuit and rolled her eyes in delight before continuing. "And yes, this morning was no exception. We had a full council meeting on Wednesday; went on for a couple of hours, it did."

"Some of the councillors like the sound of their own voices, do they?"

"My dear, I couldn't possibly comment." She winked at Celia and then carried on. "But I got everything finished and circulated just before I came across here. Twenty pages of notes, eleven copies emailed out. Not easy perched on a chair in the corner of the school office, I can tell you."

"Oh yes, of course. You've been camping in there since the leak in the village hall roof. Must be very difficult."

"Indeed. I'll be very glad when we finally raise the money to get the roof repaired and I can return to normal. Are you looking forward to the Summer Social up at the manor next Sunday?"

"I am, Miss Hillson, yes. And since Olga persuaded me to run the tea tent, I'm going to be baking every evening this week to build up stocks for that."

"And I'll be taking the money at the gate." Roger had finished serving his customers and had come through to the café to collect his coffee. "So you can be assured it will be well looked after."

"I'm delighted to hear it." Miss Hillson finished her coffee and brushed a few crumbs delicately off the front of her jacket. "Thank you, Celia my dear. That's fully refreshed me. I'm off home to dead-head my roses. I have so many, it's almost impossible to keep up with them. And of course, I need to get my outfit ready for tomorrow's service. Can't risk being late for the vicar, can I?"

As the door swung gently closed behind the upright figure, Celia smiled at her husband.

"She's such a character. And the Parish Council is really lucky to have her. You know, I don't believe she takes anything like what she's owed for doing the clerk's job. Someone said she only claims five hours a week. And I know for a fact she spends far more time than that in that little office."

Roger nodded. "But she does make me laugh. To hear her talk about getting her outfit ready for tomorrow morning's service, you'd think she had a whole wardrobe of clothes to choose from. While everyone knows she only has those three suits. Always has."

"Yes, I remember. Even when we were at school. Blue check on Mondays to Wednesdays; green check on Thursdays to Saturdays. And that special red and black check for Sundays. And always a hat to match. It's amazing. She never seems to feel the heat. Never changes her routine come rain or shine."

Celia took their mugs and popped them in the dishwasher together with Miss Hillson's cup, saucer and plate. "She was a funny old stick even then. Although I guess she wasn't that old when we were at school."

Roger put a finger to his cheek. "Let's see, she retired around ten years ago if I remember rightly, so that would make her seventy-five or thereabouts. She's thirty years older than us. She must have only been thirty-five when we were in her class."

"And I guess to a little child, anyone over twenty seems ancient." Celia looked across the road, but Miss Hillson had already disappeared. "Funny old stick or not, I still say the Parish Council – and the village – is lucky to have her."

CHAPTER 2

Josephine Hillson straightened from where she was bending over her rose bush, and stretched her back to get rid of the kinks. She wiped the back of her wrist across her damp forehead and blew a stray curl out of her eyes. It was a warm day. So warm, she was tempted to remove her heavy jacket and roll up her sleeves. But no, someone might call in unexpectedly and it wouldn't do to see the retired schoolteacher looking less than her respectable self. She decided she'd spend just another thirty minutes deadheading her roses and then she'd stop for some tea. She'd been at it for a couple of hours now. Although at this time of year, that was hardly enough to make a dent in the number of faded blooms needing to be removed. Josephine loved her garden, taken over from her father when he was no longer able to look after it himself, and roses were indeed one of her favourite flowers. But just occasionally, she wished he'd specialised in something less needy.

As she bent to her task once more, she heard voices coming up the lane towards her. She moved closer to the wall, to make it easier to listen to the conversation. It sounded like a couple of youngsters.

"It'll be a doddle. It's only Roger Richardson from the café. And he's easy to prank. It's not as if it'll be the first time."

"I'm not sure. Suppose we get caught?"

"Why should we get caught? You'll chat to him about something to keep him distracted, while I sneak the box off the side of the table. You can even help him look for it when he realises it's gone. That way he'll never suspect you – or any of your friends – of being involved."

"And you reckon there'll be lots in there?"

"Bound to be. It says on the poster it's a pound to get in. And they reckon all the village will be there. So if we leave it until later in the day, we can be sure of getting a good hundred quid in there. Maybe even more. Certainly enough to give us a good summer this year."

The voices started to fade as the boys walked past. Josephine risked poking her head above the rose bushes to see if she could confirm her suspicions. And sure enough, the red and green hoodies gave it away. The Worcester twins were up to their tricks again.

Well, she'd see about that. Okay, so it wasn't the crime of the century. And from the sound of it, the pair were setting their sights pretty low. In fact if they really wanted a decent haul from their theft, the tea tent takings were a much better bet. But that wasn't the point. The village was coming together to raise money to repair the roof of the village hall. A roof she desperately wanted to see back in one piece. And if Josephine had anything to do with it, no young teenagers with too much time on their hands were going to spoil things for the rest of them.

As she continued to snip with her secateurs and the pile of dead flowers in her trug grew to such a point that it threatened to spill over onto the lawn, she considered her options.

She could tackle the twins herself. In her many years teaching, she'd had plenty of experience facing up to naughty children. There had been very few who were willing or able to defy Miss Hillson at her strictest. But those had always been primary school children. They had to crane their necks to look her in the face. And it was much harder to be defiant when looking up at someone. The twins were sixteen, going on seventeen, as far as she knew, and taller than her. She wasn't sure she would have the same air of authority in this case.

She wondered if she should talk to Olga Mountjoy. After all, she was the principal organiser of the event. No, that wouldn't be fair. She had far too much on her plate at the moment.

Maybe she could have a word with Roger Richardson. Tell him she thought there was a plot to purloin the cash box and leave it to him to be on his guard. But then, if he did succeed in stopping the twins getting away with it, would that just put all the other cash boxes at risk? After all, there would be people collecting money all over the grounds that afternoon. Plenty of targets for the boys to attack.

No, there was only one sensible approach, reluctant as she was to take it. Josephine had always believed that the responsibility for a child's behaviour began in the home with the parents. And even though she knew the Worcester home life was far from ideal, she knew what she had to do.

Her extra thirty minutes were up and her trug was completely full. Josephine emptied the dead blooms into the compost bin and gave it a quick stir. She wiped and dried her secateurs and hung them on their hook in the little shed at the bottom of the garden. Then she returned to the house, leaving her gardening shoes in the scullery and washing her hands in the kitchen sink. As she waited for the kettle to boil, she consulted the village directory, finding the name she needed under W, and reached for the phone.

"Hello?" Josephine was relieved to hear a female voice answer the phone rather than a young male one. "Caroline, it's Josephine Hillson here. There's something I think you should know."

CHAPTER 3

Josephine Hillson snuggled back into her recliner and stretched her legs out in front of her, wriggling her toes and squeezing her fingers into fists. She yawned noisily, in a way that would have earned any of her former pupils a quick tweak of the ear. Then she settled her feet comfortably on the footrest and adjusted the angle of the chair-back so it was perfect for watching television.

It had been a long day, but she'd be able to tick off most things on her To Do list when she checked it in the morning. She'd put in a good morning's shift in the clerk's office, including drafting a response to that Fenella Sunderland about her plan for a new gym.

Such a ridiculous idea. Who'd want lots of folks in cars driving into the village at all hours to spend time pounding a treadmill, when they lived in the middle of the countryside and there were free walks available right on their doorstep. Josephine was so glad she'd managed to steer last week's Planning Committee meeting in the right direction. Of course, she hadn't said anything that could be traced back to her. It wasn't her place to have opinions. But a word or two in the right ears was all it took. No, she didn't think they'd be hearing any more about that project.

Then she'd had a delightful chat with that nice Celia

Richardson in the café. Always been a favourite of hers, had Celia – right since the days she'd sat in the front row of her classroom. Thirty-five, no it must be forty, years ago now. Josephine had been a bit worried in those days about how close Celia and Roger were. It hadn't seemed healthy in children that young. Josephine had predicted there'd be upsets when they got older – and for a while she'd been right, when Celia got swept along by the whirlwind of Sidney Wentworth. But that turned out to be a flash in the pan and Josephine had to admit the Richardsons seemed as happy in each other's company today as they had in the classroom. And they'd certainly made a pretty good job of running the café for years now, ever since Celia's parents had retired. So that was alright.

As Josephine reached for the remote control and that week's *Radio Times* – she'd stuck with that publication even after all the main newspapers started publishing their own TV listings – she reflected on the conversation she'd had a couple of hours ago with Caroline Worcester. Another familiar face from years ago, Caroline was struggling to bring her twin boys up well since their father had abandoned them all and run off with a market researcher he'd met at a conference in Exeter. Josephine knew Caroline was doing her best, but she was working two jobs to hold the little family together and couldn't keep as close an eye on the twins as they needed.

Caroline had been mortified to hear the boys had been planning to rob the takings from the Summer Social. She'd promised to talk to them immediately and, without naming names, make it clear they'd been overheard, and their plan was exposed.

"Don't worry, Miss Hillson." Caroline, like many of Josephine's former pupils, never lost the formality in addressing their old teacher. "I've got just the thing to keep those boys of mine out of trouble. They've been training as lifeguards and have been doing regular shifts over at Chudleigh this summer. I happen to know Olga's looking for some help at the pool up at the manor on Sunday afternoon, so she can open it up to the kids during the Summer Social. I'll give her a ring and tell her she has a couple more volunteers."

Yes, all in all, Josephine thought it had been a most productive day. She patted her lap. Tiger, her large, orange-striped tomcat, needed no second invitation. He leapt up onto her knees, turned twice in a circle and settled himself down with a sigh.

But as Josephine opened the *Radio Times*, the phone rang. She picked up the old-fashioned black receiver and put it to her ear. The voice at the other end was male, harsh and not immediately recognisable.

"We know what you're doing, you old witch."

"I beg your pardon, young man?" As a former schoolteacher, even a highly-respected one, she was used to the occasional verbal attack. But even as Josephine tried to remain calm, she felt a frisson of fear. "Who is this?"

"Never you mind who this is. We just wanted you to know you can't hide for ever. We're watching you and you're going to have to pay for what you're doing."

"I'm sorry, sir, but you must have me mixed up with someone else. My conscience is completely clear. Good evening to you." The receiver was not exactly slammed back into place. Josephine would never do anything so unladylike. But after it struck the cradle with a solid crack, she continued to stare at it, musing on the brief call.

She'd addressed her caller as "young man" out of force of habit but now she thought about it, she really couldn't tell whether she'd been talking to a teenager or someone much closer to her own age. And as for his claim to "know what you're doing", that could mean anything. He hadn't called her by her name, so she had no idea whether he really was calling her, whether it was a case of mistaken identity, or just the ravings of a random mischief maker.

But deep down, she knew he would have been able to give her name, if he'd been pushed. And she had a pretty good idea what he was talking about, too. She wondered which of the people listed in her little green book had decided to develop a backbone.

"Looks like we're in for some fun, Tiger." She stroked the thick orange fur and was rewarded with a deep rumble of pleasure from the dozing cat's throat. "I think it's time for another round of letters. Let's see if we can bring my mystery caller out into the open."

But as Josephine switched on the television and settled down to watch the latest goings-on in Holby City Hospital she didn't feel quite as relaxed as she had a few moments before.

CHAPTER 4
SUNDAY 25ᵀᴴ AUGUST

"Good morning, Melanie, it's lovely to see you. And Edward's home too. How wonderful." The Reverend Rosemary Leafield felt a warm glow at the thought of how good her choir was going to sound this morning. Not only was Melanie Jennings their strongest alto, but her husband of twelve months was a professional opera singer. "Go on in. The vestry's open. I'll join you in a little while."

Reluctant to enter the cool gloom of the church on such a bright sunny morning, Rosemary tilted her face to the sun and continued to greet her parishioners as they strolled up the path in ones and twos. And looking towards the village green, she spotted the one parishioner in particular that she was hoping to see.

Josephine Hillson stepped through the lychgate, back straight, stride purposeful. She was wearing her customary Sunday best, a red and black check suit. Someone had suggested to Rosemary that the retired teacher had once had a Scottish lover and had dressed accordingly ever since, but Rosemary didn't believe that for one moment. Today, the suit was accessorised with a straw hat and white lacy gloves, presumably in acknowledgment of the season. As someone who often found herself wearing unseasonably heavy clothing, Rosemary wondered how Josephine managed to always look so cool.

"Good morning, Reverend." Josephine was carrying her old leather prayer book, its creased spine witness to the many years it had attended the worship not only of its current owner, but also her father and grandfather before her, as she'd once told Rosemary. "Were you waiting to see me?"

"Yes, Josephine, I was." Rosemary's dual position within the community, both as vicar and current Chair of the Parish Council, was such that she had no compunction about using the other woman's first name, even though it usually resulted, as it did now, in a twitch of a carefully outlined eyebrow. "I just wanted to touch base about next month's Parish Council meeting. I know next year's budget isn't due for a couple of months yet, but knowing how difficult it's likely to be, I thought we might start the ball rolling with an informal discussion. Just to see where everyone's coming from, as it were."

"Excellent idea. I was going to suggest exactly the same thing." Josephine pushed her prayer book under her arm and pulled a tiny notebook and pencil out of her pocket. "I'll make a note now and amend the agenda when I'm in the office tomorrow." Note made, she popped the notebook away and smoothed the side of her already immaculate hair with one gloved hand. "Well, mustn't keep Our Lord waiting, must we?"

Rosemary stood back and waited for the older woman to precede her into the vestibule and through the inner doors into the interior of St Rumon's. She watched as Josephine strode up the middle aisle and stopped at the sixth row from the back. Without being able to see the detail, Rosemary knew exactly what would happen next.

Bending down, Josephine unhooked an embroidered kneeler from the back of the seat in front. Rosemary could describe the kneeler with her eyes closed; it always took pride of place at every craft exhibition the church or the village put on. Delicately illustrated with the date, 2002, crowns and corgis in metallic thread, it had been produced to celebrate the late queen's Golden Jubilee, long before Rosemary had come to Coombesford or even been ordained. Josephine was rightly proud of her needlework, although Rosemary had never seen her with a needle or thread in her hand.

As Rosemary watched, the elderly woman knelt, making her the only member of the congregation to do so. She buried her face in her hands and leaned forward, with a slight rocking motion. A couple stopped by her pew and looked as though they were about to disturb the praying woman, but obviously thought better of it and, with a shrug and an indulgent smile, took their seats in an empty row across the aisle from her.

Rosemary checked her watch. Ten minutes until the service was due to start. She made her way to the vestry to finish her preparations. There was quite a good crowd this morning. It must be the sunshine that was bringing them all out. Or maybe the fact that next Sunday the church would be empty, as everyone would be getting ready for the Summer Social.

That was another thing she had to remember to do. Check with Olga on how the money from the event was going to be handled. The fundraiser was in aid of the village hall roof. Was there any way they could increase the amount raised by claiming Gift Aid? Finance was not one of Rosemary's strengths. She always relied on her Treasurer for advice in that direction. And Josephine Hillson of course.

Glancing back down the church before entering the vestry, Rosemary saw Josephine had now finished her entry prayer. She'd taken her seat and was turning the pages of her prayer book, as she must have done so many times before. A bit of an old fogey, as Rosemary's mother used to say. But such a devout woman. And so dedicated to her job as clerk to the Parish Council. They were so lucky to have her. And Rosemary decided she needed to make sure the other woman knew just how appreciated she was.

CHAPTER 5
MONDAY 26TH AUGUST

If Josephine Hillson had been concentrating, she would never have been caught unawares. But the strange phone call on Saturday night, with its sinister undertones, had left her in a whirl. Even her customary Sunday morning worship had failed to quiet her mind.

So when Olga Mountjoy rapped her knuckles on the door jamb and breezed into the room without waiting to be given permission to enter, she took Josephine completely by surprise. Dropping the file she'd been reading as though it had suddenly become burning hot, she slammed the filing cabinet drawer closed and spun to meet her visitor. Unfortunately, she failed to move her left hand quickly enough and her fingers were caught by the heavy metal like a closing jaw.

"Ouch. Oh. Oh my goodness." Josephine clutched her burning fingers to her chest and sat down hurriedly as a wave of dizziness threatened to overwhelm her. She realised her legs were trembling and she bit her lip to prevent herself from crying.

"Miss Hillson. Are you alright?" Olga ran across the room and stooped down in front of Josephine, concern written all over her face. "I'm so sorry. I didn't mean to startle you."

"It's alright, my dear." Josephine took several deep breaths and waited for the pain to subside. "It wasn't your fault. It was my own carelessness." She held out her hand and was pleased to note there was barely a tremor. "And see, it didn't even break the skin. Although I suspect there's going to be a nasty bruise in a little while."

"Yes, I think you're right." Olga stood up. "But if you don't need any immediate first aid, let me make you a cup of tea. It's the least I can do." She looked around the small room. "Don't you have a kettle in here?"

Since the village hall had developed a leaking roof towards the end of the previous year, the Parish Council had been meeting in the primary school hall, and a small room to the side of the stage had been loaned to them as an office. There was barely room for a desk, two chairs and a couple of filing cabinets.

"Not in here, no. There isn't room. But we're allowed to use the staffroom kitchen." Josephine pointed to a bunch of keys on the desk. "The door's locked as it's the holidays. It's the one with the orange fob."

"Okay. One milky tea coming up, with lots of sugar." Olga smiled as she paused in the doorway. "It's what my gran always prescribed for shock. I won't be long."

As she listened to Olga's high-heeled mules clip-clopping down the hallway, Josephine wondered how she'd missed the other woman's arrival. She really must have been deep in thought. Mind you, when she considered the file she'd been reading, it was hardly surprising. But she'd think about that later, when her visitor had gone.

Josephine leaned back in the chair and closed her eyes. The sharp pain in her hand had given way to a dull throbbing ache. She wondered if she'd got any paracetamol in her bag. Or maybe in the desk drawer. She'd get up and check in a minute or two. Or maybe she'd ask Olga to check for her…

"Miss Hillson. Miss Hillson." Josephine opened her eyes with a start and pulled back in shock. Olga Mountjoy was leaning over her with a look of complete panic on her face. She was so close that Josephine could see every detail of the tiny diamond stud on Olga's nose, and the faint signs of age beginning to appear as laughter lines around her beautifully made-up eyes.

Josephine pulled herself up straight in her seat. "I'm so sorry, my dear, I must have dozed off."

"That's fine. I was just worried when I didn't get an answer straight away." Olga turned to the desk and pointed to a heavy mug sitting on the centre of the blotter. "I'll leave your tea there, shall I?"

Josephine shuddered inwardly. She hated drinking out of a mug. She should have told Olga where to find her own cup and saucer, brought specially from home. But she knew the other woman was just trying to help. And she was a foreigner, when all was said and done. No matter who she'd married, her roots were still in a very different culture.

Josephine reached over and picked up the mug, taking just a sip to test the temperature. Then she gave herself a mental shake and smiled up at her visitor.

"This is very kind of you, Mrs Mountjoy. But I'm sure you didn't come over here just to run around after an old woman. What can I do for you?" The parish clerk was back in the room.

Josephine listened to Olga's questions relating to the fundraising event taking place the following weekend and answered them one by one.

Yes, she could confirm the insurance policy was up to date.

Yes, she'd spoken to the printers, and the programme would be delivered on Thursday afternoon.

No, she hadn't forgotten that the Chair would need her chain for the opening ceremony. In fact, Rosemary Leafield already had it at home with her.

Within a few moments, the queries were all dealt with.

"To be honest with you, Miss Hillson, I'm a bit overwhelmed by all of this." Olga took a tiny scrap of material from her sleeve and held it delicately to her eyes. "Simon was so much better at this sort of thing than me."

Frankly, Josephine didn't believe a word of it. She could see the other woman was thoroughly enjoying being the centre of attention in this way. But if it helped get the roof mended and Josephine was able to get back into her own office and out of this horrible little room, then Olga Mountjoy was welcome to play lady of the manor to her heart's content.

CHAPTER 6

Rohan Banerjee had served the few early customers and was just about to check on the bookings for the restaurant when the outside door opened and a small black and white bundle of fur flew across the room and skidded to a halt in front of the bar, tail quivering.

"Hello, Bertie." Rohan came round to the front of the bar and bent down to give the squirming little dog a hug. "How's Olga treating you, then?"

"Olga's treating me very well, thank you for asking." The voice above his head sounded amused. "I have lots of space to run around in and all the treats I can eat!"

Rohan gave Bertie a final pat and stood up, grinning at Olga who was standing in the middle of the bar with her hands on her hips.

"And all I ask in return is that he keeps an eye out for rodents under my shed." Olga climbed up onto one of the bar stools. "Vodka and tonic please, Rohan, and one for yourself." She looked around at the empty bar. "It's a bit quiet in here, isn't it?"

"Always is on a Monday." Rohan poured their drinks. "But, we were busy over the weekend, so Charlie and Annie won't be complaining about a fall in takings when they get back from honeymoon."

"But that's not going to be for a while yet. They've only been gone a couple of weeks. Have you heard from them?"

"Once or twice. Although actually, it's mainly WhatsApp messages from Suzy."

"Yes, I've heard from her too. Worried about whether Bertie's pining without her."

The Jack Russell was curled up on the floor below Olga's stool. At the sound of his name, he opened one eye and cocked an ear. Rohan leaned across the bar and stared down at him.

"Well, the poor little chap must be feeling a bit confused about things. First he loses Henry Whitehead and has to get used to living with a new family here at the Falls."

"Although he seemed to settle in very well," Olga said. "He and Suzy bonded straight away."

"And now Suzy's disappeared to Latin America with her mothers and left him with another stranger."

"Hardly a stranger, darling." Olga looked quite miffed for a moment. "Suzy's brought him round to me so often lately, he thinks Mountjoy Manor is his second home." She took another sip of her drink and fixed Rohan with a stare. Oh-oh. He knew what was coming next. "And talking of second homes, how's life suiting you up at Steele Farm?"

"Very well indeed." Rohan nodded. "In fact life's a lot less stressful all round. Farmer Steele's treating me very well."

"And I guess it's much better than commercial renting?"

"Definitely. My digs are far bigger and I have work space as well, but it's less than I was paying for that awful room in Teignmouth." Rohan checked to make sure there was no-one waiting for a drink before continuing. "In fact, life's a lot less expensive all round. I can walk here or to the café. And if I need a car for a job, Tommy lets me borrow one of the farm vehicles. So I'm quids in, actually."

"And what about the lovely Esther?" Olga raised an elegant eyebrow at him. "How's she treating her new lodger?"

"Esther is a wonderful landlady." Rohan could feel himself flushing bright red, and grabbed a cloth to wipe down the bar. "And an accomplished cook as well."

"Oh, darling, I'm sorry. I've embarrassed you." Olga's laugh was warm and throaty. Rohan suspected she wasn't sorry at all. But he didn't know exactly where he stood with Esther Steele and he wasn't ready to discuss the situation with anyone else.

"I had a strange little incident this morning." Olga was making an obvious effort to change the subject, for which Rohan was grateful. "I popped into the school to have a chat with Josephine Hillson."

"The school? But isn't it shut for the summer?"

"Yes, the school is, but the temporary council office is open every morning."

"Oh yes, of course. I'd forgotten that. And how was she?"

"Actually, that's what was so strange. When I went in, she was standing at the filing cabinet reading from one of the folders. In fact she was so engrossed, she didn't seem to hear me until I knocked on the open door to announce myself."

"What's strange about that? It's easy to get so engrossed in something that you switch off from everything else." Rohan shrugged. "I know I do it all the time."

"Yes, of course. But it was her reaction when she finally heard me that was strange." Olga put her head on one side, as though considering how to put her thought into words. "You know how calm and dignified she normally is?" Rohan nodded. "Well, this time, she was anything but. In fact, she jumped as though someone had caught her with her hand in the cake tin."

"I think you mean cookie jar." Rohan grinned. "And what happened next?"

"She dropped the folder as though she'd been scalded and slammed the drawer shut. So much so that she actually caught her fingers as it closed."

"Ouch."

"Indeed. She was pretty shaken up, to be honest. I made her a cup of tea and when I brought it back, she seemed to have dropped off to sleep. I had quite a job waking her up."

"Did you get any explanation from her?"

Olga shook her head. "None at all. In fact, once she'd had her tea, she was back to normal, her usual efficient self. Didn't mention the incident at all, although she thanked me for the tea."

"Well, I doubt if it was anything suspicious. You probably just made her jump." Rohan put his drink to one side and went to serve a newly-arrived customer. "After all," he said when he returned, "I can hardly imagine the esteemed Miss Hillson getting involved in anything dodgy. Can you?"

CHAPTER 7
TUESDAY 27ᵀᴴ AUGUST

Josephine Hillson woke with a sore hand and a stiff neck. It appeared her mishap with the filing cabinet had affected her slightly more than she'd anticipated. In fact as she stared at the bedside clock, whose hands indicated it was well past her normal rising hour, she felt for the first time in a very long while that she couldn't be bothered. She couldn't be bothered getting up, washing and dressing. She couldn't be bothered collecting her briefcase from its usual resting place beside the front door. And she certainly couldn't be bothered going into the tiny room in the deserted school and toiling over council papers.

In fact, if it hadn't been for Tiger, she would probably have pulled the covers over her head and gone back to sleep. But her orange tomcat had different ideas.

First he tried pawing at the duvet where it just skirted the floor at the side of the bed. Then he tried mewing plaintively. And when that didn't work either, he jumped up onto the bed and made a nest for himself on Josephine's chest. Which, of course, involved walking around in circles several times, punching the bedclothes with his paws, and then throwing himself down with his tail wrapped across her face.

At which point, Josephine burst out laughing. "Alright, Tiger, I get the message." She pushed him to the ground, threw back the duvet and grabbed her summer-weight dressing gown from the chair in the corner. And as she walked downstairs she thanked God, for the umpteenth time, for the old couple who'd asked her to take one of their kittens five years back.

But as she sipped her tea and watched Tiger devour his breakfast, she came to a decision. She still didn't feel like going into work. She was going to award herself a day off. And she wasn't even going to get dressed. At least not yet.

She cut herself a couple of slices off a fresh loaf she'd taken from the freezer the night before, lightly toasted them and spread them thickly with golden butter. Placing them on a tray with a dish of marmalade – even now, she could hear her mother saying "never put a jar on the table, Josephine, it's so common" – and a refreshed pot of tea, she headed for her study. Located at the back of the house, and not overlooked in any direction, that was the only room where the windows weren't swathed in pristine net curtains. Facing south-east, it was flooded with sunlight, glinting off her collection of cut glass animals and spreading pools of liquid gold across the light coloured carpet.

Josephine gave a deep sigh of pleasure as she placed the tray on the small side table and sank into the only chair in the room, a highly polished leather recliner which allowed her to either sit up to the table, or stretch out and relax, as the mood took her. There was only that one chair; she only ever needed one. Josephine had never invited anyone into her study – and she couldn't conceive of a situation where she might wish to do so. This room was her haven, the one part of her life that she had never shared with anyone at all.

The original fireplace was still there, black cast iron grate surrounded by butter yellow and marbled green tiles. Central heating having long ago dispensed with the need for a real fire in any part of the cottage, Josephine had filled the grate with pine cones. A large vase of golden rod stood on the hearth.

Either side of the fireplace, the alcoves were filled with shelves. On the right-hand side were Josephine's favourite books: her leather-covered Dickens collection plus other eighteenth- and nineteenth-century authors she returned to time and again.

But it was to the left of the fireplace that her gaze turned on this morning of unexpected – and therefore delicious – free time. Three shelves of magazine file holders, filled with scrapbooks, each with a year printed carefully on the spine. Stretching back more than sixty years, the numbering was initially childish, highly coloured and slightly wobbly. As the years progressed, the colours quietened down, and the lines became straighter.

Josephine knew her scrapbooks were an extraordinary accumulation of memories. She also knew that one day, they would be seen by other people, and would hopefully be deemed an historical collection any local museum would be glad to have. But she suspected they might just be dismissed as the anachronistic habit of an old woman. Whatever the future brought, they were, for the moment, her secret. And at times, if she felt lonely or dispirited, she would take one down from the shelf and relive former happy days.

The scrapbooks took up the top three shelves. Below them there was a shelf of trays filled with all sorts of stationery items: scissors, glue sticks, rulers, pencils and pens in every possible colour. Plus a stack of plain cream writing paper and matching envelopes. And on the floor, in a large basket, a stack of magazines, and newspapers.

Josephine knew the contents of that basket would surprise, maybe even shock, anyone who went through it. Broadsheets to the right of the political spectrum, those would be quite understandable, expected even, in the home of the retired schoolteacher. Colour supplements from the weekend equivalent also. But the latest in gossip magazines and publications dedicated to television soaps, now that was out of character. But for her purposes, they were perfect.

And it wasn't as though she ever read any of the articles. She was only interested in the headlines.

Finishing her toast and marmalade, she wiped her fingers clean on a napkin and glanced across at Tiger who had made himself comfortable in the largest spot of sunlight on the carpet. "Right, Tiger, let's get started, shall we." And Josephine hummed a little tune to herself as she picked up a recent copy of *Heat* and reached for her sharpest pair of scissors.

CHAPTER 8
WEDNESDAY 28TH AUGUST

"Looks like it's going to be another hot one, Lindy." Olga Mountjoy unlocked the glass bifold doors running across the width of the kitchen and pushed them wide open. "I'll take my tray out on the terrace."

"Right you are, ma'am." Lindy Price clicked the switch on the kettle and popped a couple of slices of fruit loaf into the toaster. She'd been working at Mountjoy Manor for nearly five years now and didn't need to ask what her boss wanted for breakfast. In fact, the tray was already laid out when Olga climbed the stairs from the pool room, following her early morning swim. Fifty lengths every morning without fail.

Olga settled herself at the table on the terrace and picked up the notebook that had almost become an extension to her arm in the past few weeks. She yawned as she flipped it open and stared at the long list she'd written earlier in the week. Some of the items were ticked and crossed through. But far too many remained undone.

She'd been happy to agree to the request from the Parish Council to host the Summer Social as a fundraiser for the village hall roof. In fact, given her intention to stand for council herself at the next election, she'd jumped at the chance to win some brownie points. Brownie points – what a quaint saying. She must remember to ask someone where it came from. Celia, she would know.

So no, she didn't regret getting involved, but it had started as a modest proposal and gradually grown into a huge project. And it was this Sunday. Where had the time gone? There were only four more days before it all had to be ready.

And that reminded her. Saturday was changeover day. She'd be far too busy to greet her new guests herself. She reached over and touched her housekeeper's arm as she placed the tray on the table.

"Lindy, are you okay to do the usual couple of extra hours this weekend? On Saturday afternoon. I won't be here when the Airbnb guests arrive."

Simon would have been horrified at the idea of paying guests in his beloved family home, but it was such a huge place for just one person. Olga had converted part of the upper floors into two self-contained units a couple of years previously and the chance to stay at a real manor house in a pretty Devon village was proving very popular, especially with American visitors.

"That could be difficult, ma'am. I've got the cleaners coming in to do the changeover as usual but I promised Celia I'd do some baking for the cake stall."

"Well, why don't you do that here?" Olga looked around the luxurious kitchen. "You've got all the equipment you need, and you know how the ovens work. That way, you could meet the guests – and maybe give them a couple of scones for tea, as a welcome."

"Sounds like a plan." Lindy smiled and nodded. "And I can leave everything here when I'm finished, save carrying it all over on Sunday morning."

"Great, that's settled then." Olga picked up the serrated spoon and attacked her grapefruit. "And I'll be around somewhere if you need me. I'm just not sure where."

From the other side of the house came the sound of

tyres on the gravelled drive, a car door slamming and then in the distance, the ringing of the doorbell. Olga looked at her watch. "Sounds like the post. He's early. Would you mind answering the door, Lindy?"

It was actually a rhetorical question. Olga knew very well that Lindy had been listening out for the sound of the postman's van and would be only too happy to open the door to the shy young man who would hand over a pile of letters with downcast eyes and then stand shuffling his feet, trying to make conversation with her housekeeper.

Olga shook her head and smiled ruefully. She wondered just how long it would take before the pair finally acknowledged their mutual attraction and did something about it.

The conversation on the doorstep seemed to go on for longer than usual, which was a good sign, and Olga had finished her toast and was just pouring herself a second cup of tea when Lindy returned.

"And what did the handsome Brian have to say for himself today?" Olga wiped her hands and took the post from Lindy, whose colour was higher than it had been when she'd left the terrace. "Is he coming to the Summer Social on Sunday?"

"He said he might do, ma'am." Lindy shrugged. "But who knows? He's said that before about other events, and not turned up."

"Oh, I'm sure he'll be here this time." Olga grinned to herself, knowing that Postman Brian was actually on the rota for stewarding on Sunday afternoon. And she'd make sure he was working close to the tea tent.

As she flicked through the pile of letters, and discarded obvious adverts for immediate recycling, one envelope in particular caught her eye. No stamp, and just her name written in coloured pen in very shaky handwriting. It looked as if it had been written by a child. Or maybe someone using their left hand.

Slitting the envelope open, she pulled out a folded sheet

and opened it. She stared at the single sentence in silence before bursting out laughing. She threw the sheet on the table and pushed it across towards Lindy.

The housekeeper looked down at it and gasped. "What on earth can it mean?"

"What can it mean?" Olga picked it up and stared at the words on the page, all cut from different publications by the look of it: *I know what you've been doing and I know who with.* "It means someone's got too much time on their hands. This is the third letter I've had in recent weeks." She picked it up, screwed it into a ball and aimed it at the recycling box on the corner of the terrace.

And as Olga prepared to get on with her busy day, she grinned at Lindy. "They know what I'm doing, do they? And who with? Really?" She gave a throaty laugh. "All I can say is, chance would be a fine thing."

CHAPTER 9

"Good morning, good morning. Another lovely day. How's we today?" Joel Leafield beamed at his family seated around the table in the sunny conservatory they used as a dining room throughout the warmer months of the year. His wife Rosemary, dressed today in formal clothes, pale blue rather than black, but with the trademark clerical collar. And his two daughters, who seemed to have changed overnight from little girls who would vie for a place on Daddy's knee as he read them a bedtime story into young women, smart, elegant and worldly-wise beyond their years.

Yes, Joel knew he was a lucky man. A loving wife, respected by the community, and two teenagers thankfully still happy to spend time with their parents – at the moment anyway.

And to make it even better, today was Wednesday. His favourite day of the week. The day his whole family was busy with their own activities, meetings and sports clubs running late into the evening. There was no family meal at the vicarage on Wednesdays. And no-one to notice where Joel went from midday until early evening. Or who he spent his time with.

Joel popped a kiss on each daughter's head and squeezed Rosemary's hand as he took his place at the table next to her.

She was reading her Kindle, propped up against the cereal boxes, and threw him a distracted smile. "Minutes of the last meeting. Got to finish going through them before I leave for Exeter."

"Post's here, Dad." Neither daughter looked up from their phones, but a slim hand pushed a pile of letters across the table towards him. Joel wondered, not for the first time, whether he should try to institute a 'no screens at the table' rule indoors – they already had one, under protest, on the rare occasions they went out to eat as a family. But given that his wife was as big a culprit as the next generation, he guessed he'd be onto a loser there.

Hidden at the bottom of the pile, between a begging letter from a charity he'd once sent a small donation to, and from whom he received a further request at least twice a month, and a catalogue from the local garden centre, he found a cream envelope. It was unstamped and his name, written in bright green crayon, looked like something he would have tacked to the fridge years ago when the girls were at nursery school.

He pulled the single sheet from the envelope and gazed at the words scattered across the page: *I know what you've been doing, and I know who with.* His sight blurred as he realised he was in trouble. Big trouble.

With trembling hands, and now incredibly grateful for the three screens holding everyone else's attention around the table, he folded the sheet along its original creases, pushed it back into the envelope, folded the envelope in half and slid it into his pocket. He reached for the cereal box, poured himself a bowlful, covered it with milk and began eating. At the same time, he flicked through pages of brightly coloured floral displays, as though planning the raised beds around the churchyard.

But in reality, every mouthful was like sawdust. He had difficulty swallowing. And he had no idea what flowers were on offer this month. When his bowl was empty, he pushed his chair back from the table. "Have a good day, guys." There was a chorus of murmurs in response. He walked to the kitchen, popped his bowl and mug in the dishwasher and then headed outside, pulling his mobile phone from its case on his belt as he did so.

His call was answered, as it always was, on the second ring. He'd once asked her if she sat staring at the thing all day waiting for him to call. She'd denied it of course, but her rosy cheeks had given her away. At the time he'd been flattered, although lately it seemed rather pathetic. Today, he was just grateful to hear her voice.

"It's me. I can't make it today."

The howl of protest at the other end was subdued, dignified, submissive even. Like everything else she did. But it was a howl, nevertheless.

There had never been any illusions between them. At least, he was pretty certain there hadn't. She knew she was 'the other woman' and, as such had few, if any, rights. A few hours once a week. No birthdays, unless they happened to fall on a Wednesday. No Christmases or other holidays. But they made each other happy. Or at least, she made him happy. And he hoped she wasn't lying when she told him she was happy too.

But now, there was a tinge of jealousy in her voice that he'd never heard before. "What's Rosemary got you roped into today, then?"

"No, it's not Rosemary. She's off to her meeting in Exeter as usual." He paused, trying to get his words sorted out and took a deep breath. "Actually, it's not just today."

"What do you mean – not just today?"

"It means we're going to have to cool it. Just for a while." Deep down, he knew it was probably much more than a temporary break. And he suspected she did too. "I've been getting letters. No signature. But someone knows about us. And I can't afford the scandal. Not with Rosemary's position in the village."

"I see. And I understand. Your family's standing in the

village is very important. Goodbye, Joel." The line went dead, and he knew she was gone – in more ways than one.

Joel pulled the letter out of his pocket and stared at it once more. Who could she be? He didn't know why he assumed the sender was a woman. But he did. He'd ignored the first couple of letters which had been very vague. But this one was more specific. He couldn't afford to ignore it.

He resolved to find out who the sender was. And when he did, he'd make her pay for interfering in his affairs.

CHAPTER 10
THURSDAY 29ᵀᴴ AUGUST

As Josephine Hillson strolled back across the village green towards her cottage after a morning in the council office, she spotted a visitor sitting on her garden bench waiting for her. Tall and lithe with black corkscrew curls worn down to his shoulders and escaping from the black beanie hat she had not seen him without since he was a little boy. Thick-rimmed glasses: both she and his mother had tried to persuade him to wear contact lenses, but he'd shied away from having to put anything in his eyes. And faint acne scars almost invisible now on the pale skin of his cheeks above the tiny goatee beard.

"Dylan, I didn't expect you today. Have I forgotten an appointment?" She knew she hadn't but it was more polite than reprimanding him for arriving unannounced.

"Forget an appointment, Hilly? You'd never do that." The young man stood and walked towards her, stooping to give her a quick hug. "No, I just happened to be passing and thought I'd pop in and see how my old companion was doing."

"Well, you're just in time for lunch, as you no doubt realise. Go on through to the kitchen and put the kettle on. I'm just going to pick some salad leaves from the back garden."

Josephine opened the front door and stood back to let the young man enter. She stared at his back, considering why he was really here. It was rare to be 'just passing' a village like Coombesford when you lived in Totnes, worked as a wood turner on recycled timber and travelled everywhere on foot or by bicycle.

"How's Arabella?" Josephine pushed the dish of salad leaves towards Dylan as she asked the question and watched his face closely. She knew living with his mother and dipping occasionally into his trust fund didn't sit well with the young man who preferred the world to think he was not only self-sufficient, but also doing his bit to save the planet. But Arabella Prescott was a huge part of her life; Josephine owed her so much.

"She's doing fine, as far as I know." Dylan cut a chunk off the vegan cheese he'd brought with him 'as a present' but which was much more to his taste than hers. "I don't see her from one day to another. We live very separate lives, you know."

"And you're comfortable down there in the basement? I believe you've had some work done on the apartment?"

"Yes, that's right. I had the kitchen redone. I don't cook much, but it's a good investment for Mother when I move out. She'll be able to get a good rental from it."

"Not that she needs it, of course."

"Mother always needs more money, Hilly." He gave her a lopsided grin and carried on with his lunch.

"She's…" Josephine bit her lip, desperate to ask the question, but terrified of the answer she might get. "She's not drinking again, is she?"

"I don't think so." Dylan shrugged. "But you know how good alcoholics are at hiding it."

So many times they'd sat like this across a table at mealtimes. No parents around. A chance to unwind after a busy day at school. Of course he'd been much younger then.

Nine or ten, if she remembered correctly. Such a nice age. Confident enough to have opinions about everything; not yet having a teenager's natural inclination to insist on always knowing best. She'd been happy to spend time with him. And even happier that Arabella had offered her a temporary refuge when she needed it most.

In those days, he'd been relaxed, talkative. And even as a grown man, he'd always been good company. They didn't see each other more than a few times a year these days, but he was always easy to talk to.

Until today.

Today, there was a reserve about him. A sense of feeling his way. She suspected she knew what was behind it. But she decided to bide her time and see how the conversation went. And then, as they took their coffee out into the garden to enjoy the sunshine, it all spilled out.

"Hilly, I've had a very strange letter. It arrived in the post yesterday. I need your advice."

"Sounds interesting. Tell me more."

"I think it's easier if I show you." He pulled a crumpled piece of paper from his pocket and shoved it at her. Putting her coffee down on the old wooden table that he'd made for her years before, she made a point of smoothing the paper flat before reading the words: *I know what you did and it's time you paid for your sins.*

"Oh, Dylan. I'm so sorry. That's horrible. But, what does it mean?" Josephine knew exactly what it meant. How could she forget the nights spent sitting by Dylan's bed holding his hand to soothe him after his nightmares? But she didn't know how much he remembered. They'd certainly never spoken about it in the daylight, once the nightmares had faded.

"I don't know." Dylan jumped up from his seat and strode around the lawn in front of her. "I don't know what it means."

"Maybe it's only someone making mischief for the sake of it." Josephine reached out and took his hand. "Maybe it means nothing at all."

"But who would do something like this? Who knows about my brother anyway? It's more than twenty years back. I never mention him to anyone." He allowed himself to be guided back to his seat, then pulled away from her grasp and buried his head in his hands, his shoulders heaving.

There was a long silence. Finally, Dylan looked up and Josephine thought she detected a new look on his face, one of defiance.

"What are you going to do?"

"Do, Hilly? I'm going to do nothing at all. I'm going to forget all about it." He screwed up the letter into a ball. "I have no idea who this person is or what they think they know. But I'm not going to let a total stranger control my life. So they, whoever they are, can do their worst!"

CHAPTER 11

Dylan Foster had been an unexpected, although not unwelcome, visitor. His reason for appearing on her doorstep and his reaction to the anonymous message were interesting. Josephine wondered if maybe he had more of an idea of who'd sent the letter than he was admitting to. But that was a matter for another day. That evening, there was another visitor on her way to Josephine's cottage. Equally, if not more, welcome than Dylan.

Veronica Penfold was the closest unmarried Josephine had come to bringing up a daughter. The only child of Josephine's sister and brother-in-law, she'd been born just before Josephine had left Wales for teacher training college. The two had always been close and once her parents were satisfied their daughter was old enough to travel on her own, aunt and niece both looked forward to the regular holidays taken around the country, or even, occasionally, in Madrid or Paris.

Over the years, the relationship had matured into a deep friendship between equals. At least that's how Josephine thought Veronica looked at it. Josephine herself had a slightly different view on the matter and one day she hoped to be able to share that view. Not yet. The time wasn't right for that. But tonight, she was going to start sowing the seeds.

However, one look at Veronica's face as she opened the door to her told Josephine her news would have to wait.

"Veronica darling, what on earth's the matter?" Josephine pulled the other woman into the hall and hugged her. "You look like you've seen a ghost."

"In a way, I have." Veronica pushed her wheelie suitcase out of the way under the stairs and turned to face her aunt. "I've had the most terrible bus journey."

"That's a shame. But I told you I'd come and pick you up from Exeter. You didn't need to come by public transport."

"No, the bus itself was fine. And I know you don't like driving in the evenings." Veronica shook her head. "It was who was driving the bus. I couldn't believe it when it pulled onto the stand and I saw him sitting there behind the wheel."

"Oh."

Just a single word but it must have alerted Veronica that her aunt realised what she was talking about. "You knew, didn't you? You knew Mervyn Wootton was working around here?"

"Come on into the kitchen, Veronica." Josephine took her niece by the hand and tugged her gently. "I'll put the kettle on and we can talk about it. Supper's nearly ready."

Veronica followed her into the kitchen and sank onto the settle under the window. Some of the colour was returning to her face. Josephine glanced at her and wondered if maybe her niece had only been worried about her aunt's reaction. She filled the kettle, switched it on and checked the casserole bubbling in the oven. Then she turned to face Veronica.

"As you've guessed, I knew Mervyn had moved to the West Country. Like you, I first came across him driving the bus from Exeter. And, yes, it was a shock for me – well, for both of us really." Josephine paused, thinking back to that first encounter some months back with someone she'd never expected to have to see again, once the court case was finished with. "I'm not sure he recognised me at first, but when I was about to get off, I saw the penny drop."

"What did you do?"

"Nothing to start with. I just avoided using the bus for a while. Then I realised that was cowardly of me. So I went back to the bus station and chatted with one of the staff." She winked at Veronica. "It's surprising what you can find out if you pretend to be a helpless little old lady. I learned which route he was on that week and when he was expected to go off shift. Then I hung around and spoke to him as he was leaving that evening."

"You didn't!"

"I have to say it was really scary. But I knew if I didn't do it, I would never be able to take a bus again, for fear of meeting him."

"And what did he say?" Veronica's eyes were as big and round as when her aunt used to tell her tales of dragons and knights many years before.

"To begin with, he didn't want to talk to me. But I think he was worried I was going to make a scene if he didn't. So he agreed to have a cup of tea with me."

"And…"

"And if I apologised once, I apologised ten times in the next half hour. I tried to make him see that it really had been a terrible accident. And that I was truly sorry."

"Did he accept your apology?"

"I'm not sure. I think so. I hope so. When we parted, he said he could never forget what I'd done, but he understood that without forgiveness, there would be no peace for anyone."

"Have you seen him since?"

"Once or twice, on the bus. But we've never spoken. We nod in passing and that's it." Josephine smiled. "I like to think I've made my peace with Mervyn Wootton."

By the time supper was ready and the two women sat down to eat, Veronica seemed to have fully recovered from her shock. She was much more relaxed, telling stories about the people she met through her work in the Job Centre in Cardiff.

Josephine hadn't missed the fact that when she'd said the words "what I'd done" her niece hadn't corrected her with "what we'd done". Interesting that. And slightly disappointing. Josephine decided she would hold back on her news tonight after all. She'd intended to raise the topic of her will, and the expectations that Veronica, as her only niece and closest relative, might have. But suddenly, Josephine wasn't quite so sure. She needed to think about things carefully before coming to a definite decision. Although the will was already written, and she doubted if she would be changing it. So in many ways, the die was already cast.

CHAPTER 12
FRIDAY 30TH AUGUST

"This was a brilliant idea, Cath. We must do it again." Sal Wootton picked up her knife and fork and attacked her food with relish. "In fact let's make it a regular event."

"If we do, you're going to be as big as a house come Christmas." Cath Wootton pointed to the full English on her sister-in-law's plate.

"Oh, who cares! It does you good to treat yourself once in a while." She glanced down at her svelte figure, a figure Cath would hate her for, if it was in her nature to hate anyone. "Besides, I eat so well the rest of the time, I'm sure it won't hurt me."

"And there's your running, of course. I guess, you can always go for a run later to work off all the calories."

"Only if you join me, Cath." Sal grinned. "Mind you, by the time we've walked the length and breadth of Exeter at least twice, there'll be nothing left to work off."

"Very true, Sal. Very true." Cath reached across the table to the third occupant and put her hand on his arm. "Are you alright, sweetheart? You're very quiet."

Mervyn Wootton gave a start and picked up his coffee cup. "I'm fine. Just a bit tired, is all. Didn't sleep too well last night."

"Yes, I thought you were tossing and turning a bit more than usual." Cath pointed to the two slices of toast on her husband's plate. "Is that going to be enough to keep you going until lunchtime?"

"Don't fuss, Cath. I'm just not hungry."

Cath regarded her husband thoughtfully as he chewed his toast and stared out of the window. The couple quite often went out for breakfast when he was on late shift. It was a chance to chat, away from the kids, and they usually had a great laugh. Today was different in that Sal, widow of Mervyn's brother Sean, was with them. The two women were planning a day's shopping in Exeter. But Sal and Mervyn were great pals and he never objected to her joining them. So if there was anything wrong it wasn't that. And Mervyn had barely opened his mouth since they woke up. Something was definitely not right.

"Any reason why you couldn't sleep, Merv?" Sal nudged him. "Guilty conscience? Short-changed some little old lady on the bus home maybe?" She winked at Cath. "Or maybe you're worrying about Saturday's match. The Bluebirds haven't started the season too well, have they?"

Mervyn's fingers strayed, as they always did when Cardiff City was mentioned, to the bluebird tattoo on his right arm. He shook his head.

"They'll be okay, just you see. This year, we could even be in with a shot at reaching the Premier League."

"Yeah, right." Cath was a lifelong Swansea City supporter and the couple had wrangled about the rival teams' chances throughout their married life. The only thing that united them where football was concerned was disgust over the fact that their two sons were avid Torquay fans.

"So if it's not a guilty conscience, and you're not worried about the Bluebirds, what is it?" Sal was working her way through her piled-up plate, but obviously wasn't going to let it distract her from her brother-in-law's problems. Cath would have been irritated with her persistence if she didn't want to know the answers as well.

Mervyn put down his cup and sighed, staring down at his plate. Then, as though coming to a decision, he looked up at the two women. "I saw someone on my bus yesterday. Someone from the past."

"Who, Merv?" Cath could see this was distressing him, but she needed to know.

"It was Veronica Penfold. I didn't recognise her at first, but when she got off at Coombesford, I knew it had to be her."

"Coombesford? Why Coombesford?"

"Because, Cath, that's where Josephine Hillson lives."

"How do you know that?"

"I saw her one day, months ago. She was on my bus. I ignored her, but she came back to the station a few days later and we ended up having coffee." He ran his fingers through his hair and shook his head. "It was so weird. Sitting down with the woman who caused Sean's death."

"What did she want?" Cath kept her voice quiet and steady, knowing how difficult this must be for both Mervyn and Sal.

"She wanted to apologise! To say what a terrible accident it had been. Hoped I was able to forgive her!"

"Oh, Merv. I'm so sorry. Why didn't you tell us at the time?"

"Because I wanted to put the whole encounter out of my mind. I couldn't believe she'd had the gall to approach me at all. To be honest, I just wanted to get away from her. I'd have said anything to shut her up. I told her I could never forget, and I doubted if I'd be able to forgive, but I said I'd try." He gave a little dry sob. "She even quoted the bible to me. Apparently she's become very religious in her old age."

"Well, good for her. A pity she wasn't more fond of the bible and less fond of the bottle twenty-odd years ago." Cath suddenly remembered the third member of the party and turned to her sister-in-law. "Sal, I'm so sorry. This must be awful for you."

But to her surprise, Sal calmly put down her knife and

fork and wiped her mouth with a napkin. She shook her head and smiled at Cath. "No, you're fine. I'm not upset in any way." She turned towards Mervyn. "I hated her too, her and that niece. But it's a long time ago. I still love Sean and I'll always regret the fact that we were robbed of our life together. But I've made peace with what happened. For my own sake, and for that of the kids." She placed her hand over Mervyn's. "And that's what you have to do too, Merv. Otherwise it will eat you up inside. And Sean wouldn't have wanted that."

CHAPTER 13
SATURDAY 31ST AUGUST

Caroline Worcester listened to the sounds above her head and sighed. It sounded as though two baby elephants were practising tap dancing in the bedroom. Whereas in reality, it was two teenage boys getting ready for a night out with friends. They'd been looking forward to this night all week; had hardly talked about anything else. Well, she was going to put paid to all that when they came down in a few minutes.

She'd known life was going to be very different – and difficult – from the moment the doctor told her she was expecting twins just over sixteen years ago. Of course, at that point their dad had still been around, and the young couple had looked forward to the highs and lows of family life together. But it turned out there were just too many lows for one man to cope with – or that man at least. And Caroline had been left to bring up Peter and Paul on her own.

They weren't wicked boys, not really. High spirited certainly. Always with an eye to the main chance. And very keen to earn, or otherwise obtain, spare cash whenever and wherever they could. But they never hurt anyone, and they would do anything for her. In fact, she had a sneaking suspicion that if Josephine Hillson hadn't discovered their plan and they'd gone ahead with it, they would have found some way of sharing their ill-gotten gains with her.

But Miss Hillson had heard them, and it was up to Caroline to make sure they behaved tomorrow.

There was a thundering of feet on the staircase and suddenly there in front of her were her sons. Identical twins. So difficult to tell apart that most of the time they wore colour-coded clothing: red for Peter and green for Paul. And she knew for a fact that on occasion they would swap their hoodies over. If for example one needed to raise their average mark in a subject at which the other excelled. Peter was the ringleader in everything; Paul, younger by twenty minutes, adored his brother and would do anything he suggested.

Yes, the Worcester twins were identical to virtually everyone else, but significantly different from her point of view. And she knew the key to the following few minutes lay with Paul's conscience rather than Peter's daredevil attitude to life.

"We're off, Mum." Paul moved in for a hug. Peter waved his hand and turned towards the door.

"Stop right there, gentlemen." Caroline took a deep breath and said the sentence she'd been sitting on all week, ever since Josephine Hillson's call. "You're not going anywhere. Sit down please."

"But, Mum…"

"We're going to be late…"

"I said *sit down*!"

As she looked at her two sons sitting on the edge of the sofa, poised to spring up as soon as she released them, she saw contrasting emotions on their faces. Peter was defiant and impatient. Whatever she wanted to say, he would listen, but only because he had to. Paul's face, on the other hand, was tinged with guilt. He maybe even suspected what she wanted to talk about. She sat down opposite them and smiled.

"I want to talk about tomorrow's Summer Social." Bingo! Peter's face became closed and wary. Paul had a faint rosy glow. "You know how important it is to the village, don't you?"

"Yes, Mum."

"We could hardly miss it. It's the only thing anyone's been talking about for weeks!"

"Good. So you'll understand how disappointed the organising committee was when they heard someone was planning to rob them of the hard-earned takings." She raised an eyebrow and stared at her sons in silence for a moment. "I don't suppose you know anything about that, do you?"

"No, Mum." Peter had never had any trouble lying to her face if he needed to.

"And if you did know anything about it, you'd tell me, wouldn't you?"

"Yes, Mum, of course. Can we go now?"

"No, Peter, you may not go." She turned to her other son. "You're very quiet, Paul. Is there anything you want to say?" There was a silence. A slight movement as Peter attempted to dig his elbow into his brother's side without her noticing. "Paul? I'm waiting."

"We only wanted some spending money for the holidays." Peter gave a groan and glared at Paul. But it was too late. "And we'd have given some of it to you." Paul sniffled and wiped his nose with the back of his hand."

"We're fed up with having no money!" Peter obviously realised the game was up.

"Yes, Peter, and so am I. I'm also fed up with working two jobs in order to keep this family together. But I'm especially fed up with having phone calls from people telling me my sons are misbehaving again. Mortified I was, when Miss Hillson phoned me–" Caroline broke off just before her voice became a screech. She had been determined to stay calm and reasonable. Tell them how disappointed she was. Now, she'd not only lost her temper, she'd let slip who'd snitched on them, as Peter would no doubt put it.

Caroline stood up and gazed down at the two boys in front of her. She so rarely shouted, Paul was looking crushed and even Peter seemed taken aback.

"Right, this is what's going to happen. You're not going to pinch the cash box tomorrow. In fact, I've volunteered you to help protect it. Paul, you're working on the gate with Roger Richardson from eleven to one. Then, Peter, you're taking over for the next couple of hours."

"But, Mum…"

"I've not finished, Peter. After three, you're both going to work at the pool. Olga's kindly allowing it to be open for the afternoon, but there are going to be so many kids around, she asked me to find someone sensible to make sure no-one gets into difficulty. I said I didn't know anyone sensible, but you two are trained lifeguards, so that would have to do instead."

Both boys groaned at her attempt at humour, and she wondered whether that was punishment enough and she should let them go off for the evening. But something in Peter's expression, smugness maybe, spurred her on.

"And finally, for lying to me, you're grounded for one month. Starting right now. So you'd better find something else to do this evening. You're not going to any party."

CHAPTER 14
SUNDAY 1ST SEPTEMBER

Josephine Hillson was taking a break on the terrace with Rosemary Leafield when Olga Mountjoy dropped into the chair next to them. Dressed in a tight white cropped top and matching pedal pushers, with a sparkling ruby at her navel, she looked as if she would be more at home on the Spanish Riviera than at a summer fete in an English village.

"Phew, I'm knickered." Olga fanned herself with a copy of the programme. Josephine gazed at her in disapproving silence, while Rosemary snorted with laughter.

"I think you'll find the word you're looking for is 'knackered', Olga dear." The vicar had exchanged her clerical wear for a light summer dress and looked completely relaxed. "Has Charlie Jones been teaching you slang again?"

"Actually, I learned that one from Suzy," was the amused answer, "but I seem to have got it slightly wrong."

"Yes, you certainly have. And that young lady shouldn't be using that sort of language." Josephine hadn't taken to the Ukrainian woman when Simon Mountjoy first brought her to Coombesford, and the retired schoolteacher in her still found Olga's choice of clothing less than suitable for a woman of her age – and a lady of the manor at that. But she had to admit, she was trying hard to be a useful member of the community. And she'd certainly pulled out all the stops today.

The three women had been thrown together quite a bit in the past few months, forming the main organising committee for that day's Summer Social. There'd been a lot of stress, an occasional outburst, on Olga's part mainly, but essentially they'd made a good team. And now, as the day drew to a close Josephine was satisfied they'd done the best job they could. And from the look of the crowds spending their pennies and pounds on the stalls all afternoon, it was going to be a success financially as well.

"You know," Rosemary was grinning wickedly, "if we're going to make this an annual event, we're going to have to start planning for next year pretty soon."

There was a groan from Olga. Josephine merely shuddered and held her peace. From experience, she'd be happy to get involved once she'd recovered from the exhaustion of that day, but at this moment, all she wanted to do was crawl home and hide, never getting involved in a community event – or anything to do with Coombesford for that matter – ever again.

"Sorry to disturb you, Olga," Celia Richardson leaned across the railing on the edge of the terrace and tapped their hostess on the shoulder, "but there seems to be some sort of altercation going on down at the pool, between Peter and Paul Worcester. I tried to find Caroline, but she's nowhere to be seen."

"Oh dear. What now?" Olga stretched her arms above her head then stood slowly, pushing her hands into the small of her back and arching her body to ease her aches and pains. But Josephine put up a hand to stop her.

"You stay where you are, Mrs Mountjoy. The Worcester twins and I go back a long way. I'll deal with this."

"You're a wonder, Miss Hillson." Olga sat back down with a thump. "Go through the kitchen. The inside stairs are open and it'll be quicker than going down through the garden."

Josephine crossed the terrace, entered the magnificent kitchen and took the stairs leading down one flight to the indoor pool. She could hear the shouting even before she started descending.

"It's not my fault! It was your idea!"

"And if you'd kept your mouth shut, we'd have got away with it."

"We wouldn't have got the money. We were supposed to be guarding it."

"But we wouldn't have been grounded."

There was the sound of a scuffle and Josephine rounded the bend in the stairs to see the twins engaged in a vigorous pushing match. Luckily, the pool was empty so there was no-one else to witness the scene.

"Boys, boys. That's enough!" She'd still got the teacher's voice when it was required. She'd rarely needed it with her class of primary kids, but she could remember a number of occasions when she'd had to use it on this pair. They'd been wild, even as five-year-olds. "What on earth's going on?"

The pair broke apart and turned to face her. Their cheeks were matching shades of red and they were puffing and blowing. Peter strode towards her, his finger pointing at her face.

"It's all your fault, you interfering old cow! It's about time someone put you out of your misery!"

Josephine wasn't sure whose gasp of horror was louder, hers or Paul's. But it was Paul who reacted first. He jumped forward and grabbed his brother by the arm, pulling him backwards along the side of the pool. But, failing to watch where he was heading, he veered sideways and his foot slipped off the edge. He teetered for a few seconds before toppling into the water, pulling Peter in after him.

Trained lifeguards and strong swimmers both, there was no danger in the situation, and Josephine made no effort to hide her smile of satisfaction as the pair pulled themselves out of the water and stood dripping in front of her.

"Well, I hope that's cooled your temper, young man."

She looked over her glasses at Peter, who was scowling at her, but kept his mouth shut this time. "I'll be talking to your mother next time I see her." She turned to Paul with a more sympathetic tone in her voice and held out a couple of towels. "Here. Dry yourselves off and then you'd better take your brother home."

"Yes, Miss Hillson." Paul pulled his brother by the arm, taking care to watch where he was walking this time.

As they reached the door, she heard one of them, presumably Peter, mutter something about making her sorry. But Josephine just shook her head and smiled to herself. She could handle one or both Worcester twins if she needed to. After all, they were nothing more than overgrown kids.

Looking around the empty pool house, she tutted at the state it had been left in. Damp towels were lying on several of the loungers; floats and noodles were strewn around. The clock on the wall showed it was approaching nine. The fireworks were due to start soon. She'd just have time to clear this lot up first. And that would be one less job to do later on.

It was as she was straightening the loungers and preparing to leave that she heard two things in quick succession. One was the first bang of a firework outside. The other was the sound of the upstairs door closing and footsteps coming down the stairs towards her.

CHAPTER 15
WEDNESDAY 4TH SEPTEMBER

Caroline Worcester ran a damp cloth across the draining board and work surfaces in her already spotless kitchen. She straightened the lines of spice jars sitting on the rack next to the stove. She checked the pots of herbs on the sunny windowsill had sufficient water. Then she looked around for something, anything, that was out of place and needed her attention.

But she finally had to admit there was nothing left for her to do. And she knew if she went into any of the other rooms in the little cottage she shared with her twin sons, she would find exactly the same. She'd been cleaning and polishing since dawn. Even the boys' bedroom was as neat as the day they'd moved in.

Which meant she had nothing to take her mind off the terrible thoughts she'd partitioned away under the 'too difficult to deal with' section. Thoughts that had been knocking on the partition, begging to be let out and heard. Thoughts she wouldn't, couldn't listen to.

When the news of Josephine Hillson's death had spread like wildfire across the village, she'd been shocked and saddened. She'd assumed, like everyone else, that the elderly woman had succumbed to a heart attack or similar. Maybe she'd pushed herself just that bit too hard at the fundraiser. She'd certainly seemed to be everywhere at once throughout the day.

But then yesterday afternoon came the even more terrible news. Miss Hillson, far from dying of natural causes, had been the victim of foul play. A post-mortem had confirmed that there was water in her lungs. She had drowned; and from the bruising around her arms and shoulders, it would appear she'd been forcibly held under the water.

Everyone was perplexed as to who would have wanted to hurt such a kindly, community-spirited woman. Yes, she could be a touch brusque on occasion – anyone who'd been in her class at Coombesford Primary School could attest to that. But they all agreed that she'd mellowed with age and she'd certainly thrown herself into the job of parish clerk.

So how could anyone who knew Josephine Hillson wish her harm? It must have been a stranger, just a case of being in the wrong place at the wrong time. Yet, how could a random stranger have found their way into Mountjoy Manor in the middle of a packed village event, committed murder, and escaped unnoticed?

Well, of course they couldn't. Which meant it had to be someone closer to home. And that's where Caroline's terrible thoughts were heading. She knew at least two people who weren't best pleased with the retired schoolteacher.

Neither Peter nor Paul had said anything when she'd told them of Miss Hillson's death. They'd experienced very little tragedy in real life so far and, despite their increasing exposure to death and destruction via the video games all their friends seemed to be playing, there were times when they reverted to the role of gauche young boys that she remembered so well, and mourned now that time was gone.

At least, they'd said nothing to her. She'd watched them walk across the green towards the bus stop yesterday morning talking earnestly together. Unusually, it had been Paul, her gentle supporter, who'd been doing most of the talking. Peter had shrugged and shaken his head a couple of times, but seemed to be unusually quiet. At the time, she'd dismissed the scene as just one of those moments when she was excluded, and quite rightly.

But when the news of the crime hit the village everything changed.

It was Josephine Hillson who'd reported the boys to Caroline for planning to pinch the money from the Sumer Social. And although Caroline hadn't meant to mention any names, her temper had got the better of her. So her boys knew who was responsible for the grounding they'd received, not to mention a day working as volunteers at the Summer Social.

Put that together with the fact that when the boys arrived home on Sunday evening, they were soaking wet, shivering and making a point of ignoring each other. At the time, she'd put it down to horseplay that had got out of hand, and dismissed it from her mind. But now she wasn't so sure.

Or rather, she was beginning to wonder if that's exactly what it was. She knew neither of her boys would deliberately do anything so wicked; but Peter in particular was prone to outbursts of temper when he couldn't get his own way.

And if Peter had done something stupid, would Paul, who loved his brother to the exclusion of all sense on occasion, be persuaded to cover up the crime?

The ringing of the doorbell broke into Caroline's thoughts and made her jump. As she walked to the door, she could see the outline of a slim woman through the frosted glass.

"Ms Worcester?" The woman was blonde, neatly dressed and so obviously a policewoman, that Caroline almost closed the door in her face.

"Yes. I'm Caroline Worcester."

"Ms Worcester, I'm Detective Constable Joanne Wellman." She flashed a warrant card in Caroline's face. "Can I come in?"

Caroline stepped back automatically and gestured

towards the lounge. This didn't feel like a visit she should host in the kitchen.

"What can I do for you?" Trying to sound calm and relaxed, Caroline wondered if she should show more curiosity about the purpose of the visit. A thought struck her. Maybe this was nothing to do with Josephine Hillson's death. Maybe there was something wrong – really wrong – with her sons. She felt the colour drain from her face. "My sons. Has there been an accident?" Waves of panic rolled over her.

"Nothing like that, Ms Worcester." The DC waved a hand in her direction. "I just want to have a quick chat with you." She paused and took out her notebook. "I'm sure you've heard about the body that was found in the swimming pool at Mountjoy Manor on Sunday evening."

"Miss Hillson, yes, of course." Caroline nodded.

"Well, a witness reported two teenage boys, twins he thought, coming out of the pool area around the time Miss Hillson is believed to have gone into the water. If it was your boys, it looks like they might have been among the last people to see her alive. We're hoping they might be able to give us a clue as to what happened."

CHAPTER 16

The phone rang seven or eight times before it was answered. Joel knew she'd have recognised the number and was very glad she decided to pick up at all. After last week's call, he'd assumed he'd lost her for good. There'd been something about the way she'd said "goodbye" that sounded final. And at the time, he'd been quite relieved.

But that was then. Now things were very different. Now they had a second chance. And he was going to do his best to get them back on track.

"Hello. It's me."

"Yes, I know who it is. What do you want, Joel?"

That didn't sound too promising, but Joel was a past master at talking women round. This woman in particular.

"I want you, of course. As I always do."

"Really? I thought everything was on hold. 'We're going to have to cool it' were your words, I believe. What's changed?"

"Everything, darling. Everything's changed. There's no longer any chance of Rosemary finding out. We're off the hook."

"That's nice for you, Joel. What happened?"

"I found out who sent the letters." He allowed himself a metaphorical pat on the back as he thought back to the events of the previous week.

He'd been devastated when the letter had arrived. It hadn't been the first one. There had been a couple of others in the weeks before. But they'd been harmless, and he'd dismissed them as the work of a crank. He'd thrown them away with barely a thought.

But this latest one was different. It was a letter that threatened his nice cosy position in the village, a reflection on the respect people felt for Rosemary. A letter that had temporarily sent him into a panic. But after he'd had time to think about it, he'd come to some conclusions.

The letter bore no postage stamp. So it must have been delivered by hand. And he very much doubted the writer would trust such a risky undertaking to a third party. So all he had to do was watch the post-box on the wall of the rectory garden and he would have his culprit.

Being the unofficial parish handyman, the first port of call when something went wrong in the church, meant he had picked up all sorts of knowledge and experience over the years. Including an understanding of electronics. The day the third letter arrived, he'd used the time he would usually spend with his mistress travelling to Plymouth – less chance of meeting anyone he knew – and purchased a bird cam. He'd installed it in a sheltered location further along the wall, and linked it up to his laptop. Periodically he'd run the footage at high speed but although he'd seen all sorts of comings and goings around the churchyard and the village green, there had been no-one, apart from the postman, delivering anything to the post-box.

Until the Saturday morning.

At just after five, a stout, upright elderly woman had sidled up to the wall, checked to make sure no-one was watching her – or so she thought – and then pushed a letter through the slot in the wall. As she'd hurried away, she'd briefly faced the camera full-on. But Joel hadn't needed that confirmation to know exactly who'd been interfering in his life. And sure enough, when he'd collected the bundle of post from the box later that morning, there was another unstamped envelope, addressed to him in distinctive green script, this time demanding money in return for her silence.

"So I collared her the next morning and told her the game was up." He finally paused for breath, having related the story proudly. But the reaction was less enthusiastic than he'd frankly expected it to be.

"So you've broken cover and told this Miss Hillson you're onto her." There was a cold note in her voice that Joel had never heard before. "You've not only confirmed to her that something was going on. You've shown her you're rattled." The sneer was even more pronounced. "Well done, Joel."

"But, I thought…"

"No, Joel, you didn't think, did you? What did the letter say? The exact words."

"I know what you've been doing. And I know who with." He paused as the implication of her question hit him. "Oh. I see."

"Precisely. It was a fishing letter, nothing more. No details, probably because she didn't have any. Until you went and confirmed them." There was a silence and he wondered if she'd cut the connection, but then she tutted. "You really are a very stupid man, aren't you, Joel?"

This conversation wasn't going at all the way he'd intended it to. Time to take control once more. He was beginning to get a bit tired of women taking him for a fool. He put a grin on his face and hoped it would be reflected in his voice.

"But that's not the reason I phoned you. Knowing who sent the letters is just icing on the cake. It turns out she won't be sending any more of them. To anyone. Ever."

"And how do you know that?"

"Because she's dead. The old bag was found floating face down in a swimming pool on Sunday night." He took a deep breath and felt all the fears and stress of the past week float away from him. "We're free. We can go back to normal. And I thought we'd go out and celebrate this evening. It's Wednesday and Rosemary's busy until nearly midnight."

"And so am I, Joel."

"I beg your pardon?"

"I said, I'm busy tonight."

"But it's Wednesday. You're never busy on a Wednesday."

"That was before, Joel. Before you told me we had to cool it. I didn't expect to hear from you for a while; or at all, if I'm honest."

"But the situation's changed. What are you planning to do tonight anyway?"

"That's irrelevant. I've made plans and I'm not able to change them at the last minute."

"But…"

"No, Joel, I'm sorry."

He bit back the angry words that were trying to force themselves out of his mouth. How dare she say no to him. It wasn't as though she had a lot of other options – or so he'd thought. But then he remembered what he'd risked to be with this woman – and why.

"Okay, I understand." He paused. "The usual time next week?"

"I'll ring you. I'll let you know." And this time, the silence at the other end was prolonged and he knew the call had ended.

CHAPTER 17
THURSDAY 5ᵀᴴ SEPTEMBER

"You left your purse behind." Esther ran across the green after Caroline Worcester. "Caroline, you left your purse…"

"What?" As the other woman turned, Esther gasped. The usually immaculate face looked drained, there were smudges of mascara under her eyes, and her hair didn't seem to have had a comb anywhere near it. "Oh, my purse. How silly of me." She reached out and pulled it out of Esther's hands and shoved it in her pocket. "Thanks." And turning on her heel, she resumed her rapid transit.

Esther wondered if she should mind her own business. But that thought was quickly replaced by a much kinder one. "Caroline, wait." She hurried after her friend and caught up with her just before she reached the little cottage she shared with the twins. "Are you alright?"

"Yes, I'm fine." Caroline was rooting around in her bag and finally pulled out a bunch of keys. She pushed on the heavy gate, which squeaked as it reluctantly opened.

"Well, you don't look alright." Esther placed a hand on Caroline's arm. "You look upset. Is there anything I can do to help?"

"What you can do to help," Caroline swung round to face her, eyes blazing, "is to leave me alone and mind your own damn business. The last thing I need is you interfering in my life." Then her expression changed and her hand flew to her mouth. "Oh God, Esther, I'm so sorry..." The rest of the sentence was lost in a torrent of sobs, and Caroline sagged against the gatepost.

Esther took the keys from Caroline's hands and putting her arm around her shoulder, gently guided her along the garden path. There was no resistance from Caroline as Esther opened the front door, and led her towards the kitchen.

By the time Esther had boiled the kettle, made tea and found the biscuit tin on the top shelf of the dresser, Caroline had stopped crying, although an occasional hiccupping sob still wracked her every so often and she was wringing a damp tissue so tightly it was disintegrating. Esther sat across the table and took a sip of her tea, pointing to the other mug with an encouraging smile. She'd said nothing and made no attempt to get Caroline to talk since they'd entered the cottage. Sometimes silence and a good cry was the best option.

Caroline picked up her mug, drank deeply, and then put it down with an almost steady hand. "I suppose I owe you an explanation."

"You don't owe me anything, Caroline. I saw a friend in need, that's all. If you want to talk, I'll listen. But if you'd rather just drink your tea and enjoy these delicious biscuits, that's fine by me too."

Caroline stared out of the window, biting her lip. Esther suspected whatever she was seeing, it wasn't the colourful display of roses and ox-eye daisies in the carefully tended flowerbeds.

Finally, Caroline seemed to come to a decision and turned to face her visitor. "Esther, I'm so worried, I don't know what to do. I don't want to believe it. No-one would – about their own sons. But yesterday, the police were here and they've got to be interviewed tomorrow. And I don't know what to do. I'm so scared…" Her voice dissolved into tears once more, although this time they were silent, rolling down her cheeks and dripping off her chin.

"Hold on. Start again." Esther had no idea what Caroline was talking about, apart from the fact that the twins appeared to be in trouble with the police.

"Everyone thought it was an accident, you see. And she was such a popular person. But I knew my boys…" Caroline's words faded to a halt once more.

"Are you talking about Miss Hillson?" Esther finally realised where this conversation was going. "And you think Peter and Paul…?" Caroline was nodding but Esther didn't believe it for one minute. "Go back to the beginning, will you? There must be a logical explanation for this."

Caroline took a deep breath and told Esther about the events of the previous week leading up to the twins being grounded and missing the big party. About the state they were in when they arrived back from Mountjoy Manor on the Sunday evening. About their subdued reaction to the news of the death. About her reluctant suspicions that the boys knew more than they were letting on. And finally about the visit from DC Wellman the previous evening.

"But you can't possibly think your sons are involved in Miss Hillson's murder?"

"I really don't want to." Caroline gave a deep watery sigh. "But the police obviously think they know something. That's why they want to talk to them."

"As witnesses, Caroline, as witnesses. They've not implied they're suspects, have they?"

"No, not yet." Caroline stopped and squeezed the balled-up tissue even tighter. "But what if they did? Not on purpose. I'm sure they wouldn't do that. But if Peter lost his temper…"

"Would you like me to talk to Rohan for you? He's had a lot of experience of this sort of thing."

"Do you think he'd be willing to talk to them? I'm so worried they might say something silly to the police and get themselves into real trouble."

"I'm sure he would." Esther stood up. "He's over at The Falls, managing the pub while Charlie and Annie are on honeymoon. I'll ask him."

Caroline stretched a hand out to Esther. "Will it be expensive? I don't have very much money, but I can always sell…" Her voice died away and she looked aimlessly around the kitchen as though trying to identify something of saleable value.

"Don't worry about that." Esther wasn't sure how Rohan would react if he could hear this conversation, but she couldn't bear to see the other woman in such distress. "I'm only talking about asking him for some advice. He's not going to charge you for that." She picked up her shopping bag which she'd dropped by the door when they'd arrived. "Right, I'll pop back to Cosy Café and finish my shopping and then I'm on duty in the pub kitchen. I'll talk to Rohan when the lunchtime rush is finished."

CHAPTER 18

Veronica Penfold had been sitting at the kitchen table in Josephine Hillson's house staring at the wall for a long time when something wound itself around her legs, making her start and squeal. She jumped up and peered under the table. A pair of golden-coloured eyes stared back at her from out of a striped ginger face. There was a lost look on the cat's face and he mewed softly. Veronica picked him up and rubbed her face into his fur.

"Yes, Tiger, I miss her too." She popped him down beside his dish of food and stroked his back until he settled down to eat. She took her seat at the table once more. "But don't worry. I won't leave you. I'll look after you – just as I promised her I would if anything happened…" She choked a little over the last words and rubbed her hands across her eyes.

After the ginger tom had finished eating and neatly washed his whiskers with his paws, he walked across the kitchen and parked himself in front of her, as though to say: "what are we going to do today?"

Veronica closed her eyes briefly, then gave herself a mental shake. This wouldn't do. She had to get on. She needed to meet with Josephine's solicitor, to find out what was going to happen to the house and its contents. She had a suspicion it was all coming to her. Her aunt had always implied that was the case. But until she had the proof, she couldn't do anything. And then there was the police to deal with.

Veronica had received the call from the police on the Monday morning. The terrible news that her aunt was dead. Josephine's sister, Veronica's widowed mother, lived with her daughter in Cardiff, but was too immobile to travel to Devon. And in reality, it had always been aunt and niece who were closest. For some reason there was a distance between the sisters no-one ever mentioned or tried to explain.

Arriving back in Coombesford on the Tuesday, Veronica had received the even more devastating news that her aunt had been murdered. The young police constable who'd knocked on the door that evening had told her they'd made an initial search of the house but would be returning later in the week for a more detailed investigation.

The idea of strangers going through her private property was something Veronica knew Josephine would have hated. But she knew it was inevitable. The house wasn't the crime scene – it was clear the murder had taken place at Mountjoy Manor – but there might be some clues to who hated her aunt enough to kill her.

But one thing Veronica was determined upon. She was going to go through the house today, before anyone else arrived, to make sure there was nothing her aunt wouldn't want seen. Even if it meant there was a possibility her killer would escape capture.

The kitchen yielded nothing out of the ordinary. The neatest cupboards Veronica had ever seen, tins stacked with their labels showing, everything within date. And drawers that contained only cutlery and small cooking utensils. Veronica wasn't surprised that the inevitable 'where shall I put this thing' drawer, seen in virtually every house she'd ever lived in or visited, did not exist in Josephine Hillson's life.

A similar examination of the lounge and the two bedrooms revealed the same tidy life without clutter or unnecessary belongings. The bookcase on the landing housed favourite books, obviously well-read, and shelved in alphabetical order. No scraps of paper. No piles of recipes cut out of magazines and pushed into untidy folders. Nothing.

The study was a different story altogether. Veronica had deliberately left this room until last. It had been her aunt's private sanctuary and even her favourite niece had never been allowed over the threshold. But now she was free to enter.

The first thing that struck her was the rows of scrapbooks, stretching back over the decades. A variety of shapes and sizes, but all neatly covered in colourful wrapping paper. Each one had a year neatly printed on the spine. Running her fingers along the rows, Veronica noticed a few missing years, around the turn of the century. But that was to be expected.

She pulled one off the shelf at random: 1974. Opening it, she was surprised to see her own picture looking out at her. A five-year-old child, heading off to school for the first time, a nervous grin on her face and a teddy bear clutched to her chest. Her mother was holding her hand, and her dad was waving from the front door. So who'd taken the photo? Maybe her aunt had been staying with them? She didn't remember. But why should she? It was fifty years ago, for goodness sake.

Abandoning the past, she flicked through some of the more recent ones. There were a few pictures of her, but also newspaper cuttings and photos featuring the goings-on in Coombesford. These might be useful to the police. She made a mental note to mention them.

She crossed to the bureau in the corner of the room. It was closed, but a small cream triangle poked out of the top. Opening it, she pulled out a sheet of notepaper that had got caught in the crack. Her aunt had obviously been in the middle of writing something. But how strange. There was no address or date at the top of the sheet. And although there was a name, in green ink, in the usual place for the addressee, the rest of the words were cut from a magazine and stuck haphazardly across the page.

As Veronica read the message her late aunt had been compiling, she felt herself going hot. Surely this didn't mean what she thought it did? But if it did, what was she going to do with the information? What was more important? To provide the police with clues that might lead to Josephine's killer; or to protect her reputation as a respectable retired schoolteacher and pillar of the community?

A reputation which it would appear was far from justified.

CHAPTER 19

Having spent the best part of a day sorting through Josephine's belongings and making sure there was nothing else her aunt would want kept hidden from the police, Veronica finally ran out of energy around six in the evening. She watched the *BBC News*, including *Spotlight*, but there was only a mention of the events of the weekend and the fact that the police were completely baffled.

She fed Tiger again – and worried once more about whether she'd be able to keep the old ginger tom or not – and then turned her attention to her own wellbeing. Her rumbling stomach told her she was hungry, but she had no inclination to cook, even if there was anything in the fridge or larder to suit her tastes, which she doubted.

Closing and locking the door behind her, she headed across the green and up the road to The Falls. She'd heard great things from other villagers about the local pub, although she knew her aunt hadn't been in there for the best part of twenty years.

The pub was almost empty and the Indian-looking guy behind the bar looked up and smiled as she walked through the door.

"Hi. What can I get you?"

"I'll have a diet Coke, please. And do you have a bar

menu?"

"Sure, although we've got room in the restaurant at the moment, if you want to sit at a proper table?" He pointed to the adjoining room where only two tables were currently occupied.

"No, that's fine." Veronica suddenly felt she needed company, and this cosy bar promised more than an empty restaurant. She took the menu from him and headed for a table under the window.

"I'm Rohan, by the way." The barman brought her drink across to her table. "Not seen you in here before, I don't think."

"Veronica; Veronica Penfold." She held out her hand and he shook it briefly. "I'm Josephine Hillson's niece."

Rohan's countenance changed instantly. "Of course. I should have realised. I'm so sorry for your loss." He started to move away. "I'll leave you in peace to check out the menu."

The bar seemed somehow dimmer once he'd gone and Veronica quickly scanned the menu and picked out her choices for supper. She strolled back up to the bar and placed her order. Within a few minutes, Rohan was back at her table with a plate of quiche and salad, plus a side of fresh home-baked bread and a pat of sunshine-yellow butter.

"Keep me company while I eat, if you're not too busy." Veronica looked pointedly around the empty bar.

"Happy to." Rohan grabbed a seat across the table from her. "*Bon appétit.*" He pointed to the quiche. "That's cooked by my landlady, Esther. You won't find a better pastry chef anywhere."

"Landlady? Does she run this place, then?"

"No, nothing like that." He laughed. "She helps her father run one of the local farms, and I rent a studio-cum-office from them. This place is owned by friends of ours, but they're on holiday at the moment with their daughter, so we're keeping the pub open in their absence."

He went up to the bar to serve a customer, then returned

to her table. "Must have been a nasty shock for you, hearing of Miss Hillson's death."

"Yes, it was." She struggled to keep her lips from trembling. "I've got the police coming around tomorrow to give the cottage a complete going over."

"Oh dear. Miss Hillson wouldn't have approved of that."

"Quite. In fact, I've been going through everything myself today. Just to make sure there's nothing she wouldn't want anyone to see."

"And was there anything?"

"Absolutely nothing. My aunt's life was an open book. As you would expect."

She was lying, but there was no way she was going to mention her shocking findings to this stranger. The letter had been bad enough. But when she'd found the little notebook, hidden inside one of the books on the bookcase, she'd really seen her aunt in a different light. No, she would keep those discoveries to herself until she decided whether she was going to tell the police when they came, or not.

"Do the police have any ideas yet?"

She was pulled out of her reverie by his question. "No, I don't think so. And I don't have any clues either. Although," she paused as a sudden thought struck her, "there's always Mervyn Wootton of course."

"Mervyn Wootton. Never heard of him. Who's he?"

"He's one of the bus drivers on the route from Exeter. I bumped into him when I was travelling to Coombesford last week to visit Josephine." She bit her lip, wondering where she was going with this conversation and why she was being so open with this friendly young stranger. But she realised she desperately needed someone to use as a sounding board. So why not Rohan, stand-in barman at her aunt's local pub? Not that her aunt ever went in here, of course.

She pulled a face. "Both my aunt and I knew him from years back, when we were all in Wales."

"And you didn't get on well?"

"You might say that. There was a court case, an accident. My aunt was the innocent party, but Mervyn Wootton didn't see it like that. I'd not seen him for years, so it was a bit of a shock, as you can imagine." She paused then shook her head. "I'm probably making something out of nothing, but it seems such a coincidence, seeing him here in Devon and then my aunt being killed just a few days later. Especially as, from what she told me last week, he'd been making a bit of a nuisance of himself over the past few weeks."

"That doesn't sound too good. And I don't believe in coincidences." Rohan stood up, as the door opened and a new group of drinkers entered the bar. "Look, I'll leave you to finish your supper. But if there's anything I can help you with, don't hesitate to ask. Esther, that's my landlady, and I have had quite a bit of experience at investigating murders in the past few years."

CHAPTER 20
FRIDAY 6TH SEPTEMBER

"How are you getting on in here?" It was early afternoon, the lunchtime rush had finished, when Rohan poked his head around the door of the kitchen and found Esther wiping down the surfaces. There was a gentle hum coming from the dishwasher. "Great, you're all finished. Are you okay to keep an eye on the bar for a while?"

"Yes, that's fine. Why, where are you going?"

"Only as far as the function room. I've got my laptop set up in there and I thought I'd do a bit more background research on Josephine Hillson. See if I can find anything to reassure Caroline that it was someone other than her precious twins who did the dirty on her."

"That would be good, if you could. I really can't see it myself, but Caroline was in such a state when I saw her earlier in the week, I had to offer our help." She paused. "But I thought you'd had a word with them the yesterday. Didn't you get anywhere with them?"

"Not really. I 'bumped into' them as they were coming out of the café, and tried to talk to them about Sunday, but they both clammed up and hurried off, saying they had homework to do." He shrugged. "I'll try again in the next day or so. Any news on the police investigation?"

"Apparently she went into Exeter with the boys yesterday and they answered lots of questions. Nothing to suggest they were involved, but the police said they'd be in touch again if they had any more questions and Caroline has interpreted that as them suspecting Peter and Paul might know more than they let on."

"Well, I had an interesting chat with Josephine's niece last night in the bar. She's pretty cut up, as you might imagine, but she mentioned a name, someone from their past who's been making a bit of a nuisance of himself lately. I want to see what I can find out about him."

Rohan shut himself in the function room, fired up the laptop and began hitting the keys. He couldn't find Mervyn Wootton anywhere on social media: no Facebook account, not on Twitter or LinkedIn. He didn't even bother to search Instagram or TikTok. Veronica had told him Wootton was a driver, and sure enough, on the bus company site he found reference to a winning darts team. The blurred team photograph showed Wootton to be tall, dark-haired and well-built with a rugged appearance. He appeared to be in his fifties.

Veronica had said Mervyn was Welsh and that the differences between him and Josephine Hillson stretched back to more than twenty years ago. So, he was looking for a Welsh darts player from the start of the century. And once he found one reference, the others came in thick and fast. It appeared young Mervyn had been quite the hotshot in the amateur darts leagues in his day.

But that's not all Rohan discovered. Some of the photos from back then were much clearer than the more recent one on the bus company website. They showed a young man with black hair held in place with gel, a pronounced widow's peak, and short, neat sideburns. Clean-shaven, and respectable-looking. Until you saw his arms. One bicep sported the red, white and blue of the Union flag. The other held the flag of St George within a shield. And woven around the shield were the initials BNP. Rohan's stomach quivered at the news that he was investigating a member of the British National Party. Someone who very likely wouldn't give a young detective of South Asian descent the time of day.

Yet, Mervyn Wootton was Welsh. And the Welsh were traditionally less than enamoured with the English who ruled over the principality. So what was that all about? There was obviously more to Mervyn Wootton than met the eye.

A further search, trying to link the names of Mervyn Wootton and Josephine Hillson, yielded nothing. Nor could Rohan find any mention of an accident involving Mervyn. But when it came to linking Josephine Hillson and accident, the screen just lit up.

It was back in 2001 that Josephine Hillson was involved in a car crash. A young pedestrian had been killed, and at the inquest, his family claimed it was due to dangerous driving on Josephine's part. But the police had presented evidence showing she was not at fault, and the verdict was returned as accidental death. Interestingly, a point was made in the police statement that the driver had been breathalysed and was not found to be over the limit. That seemed to Rohan like an ironic statement to make. To his knowledge, Josephine Hillson was staunchly anti-alcohol. She had certainly never stepped foot in The Falls in the years he'd been here and he'd heard from Olga that there'd been a right ding-dong between Josephine and Rosemary before the vicar got her way and had a beer tent set up for the Summer Social. Still, it was standard procedure to breathalyse all drivers involved in car accidents, so it was inevitable to find the statement there.

Realising it was getting to the time when Esther needed to start preparations for dinner, Rohan packed up the laptop and headed back to the bar to relieve her, his head whirling with what he'd discovered. It seemed as if there were still more questions than answers.

"Someone looks like they've got the worries of the world on their shoulder." It was Celia Richardson, walking down the corridor towards him. Rohan remembered she'd promised to help Esther that evening.

"Just getting my thoughts in order, Celia." He stopped as something struck him. "You've been in the village all your life. Do you remember Miss Hillson being involved in a car crash in Wales? Back in 2001, it would have been."

Celia shook her head. "Never heard a word about it. But then I wouldn't, would I? That was during her rough patch and she wasn't around here then."

"But I thought she taught you guys…"

"Oh she did. That was back in the early 1980s. Wonderful teacher, she was. Strict, but fair." Celia paused and pulled a face. "Then around fifteen years later she developed a bit of a drink problem."

"But I thought she was teetotal."

"Oh she was towards the end of her life. But for a while, she was a real lush apparently. I wasn't paying much attention to be honest. I had my own problems to deal with, as you know."

"So she left the village?"

"That's right. Gave up her job, disappeared completely for about seven or eight years, if I remember rightly. Then in 2004, her replacement retired and she came back."

"But surely if she'd had a drinking problem…"

"That's it, you see, Rohan. She had the sense to take herself away before it got completely out of hand. A few of the villagers knew, but she managed to keep it from the authorities."

As Rohan took his place behind the bar, he added Josephine Hillson herself to the list of people for whom he had more questions than answers.

CHAPTER 21

The Reverend Rosemary Leafield was sitting in the shade of the huge cypress pine in the churchyard planning her sermon for the coming Sunday when the call came in. It was a call she'd always known would come at some point, but which she'd locked up in her 'too difficult to think about' box. And even though she'd been expecting it for years – ever since Joel had started cheating on her – it still felt as if she'd been kicked in the stomach.

"Mrs Leafield." The voice was low and gravelled, as though from years of smoking. And the fact that the caller failed to use her correct title told Rosemary all she needed to know. She felt her face freeze from the welcoming smile she always adopted when answering the phone. "Mrs Leafield, you don't know me. My name is–"

"I don't need to know your name. What do you want?"

"I want to talk to you about Joel, your husband."

Rosemary wondered why the other woman felt the need to spell out who Joel was. They both knew whose husband he was. "I'm listening."

"I'm really sorry to have to tell you that Joel and I have been seeing each other."

Seeing each other. What a quaint way to describe illicit sexual encounters in anonymous hotel rooms. "Since when?"

"Pardon me?"

"For how long have you and my husband been screwing?"

There was a gasp at the other end of the phone and Rosemary wondered which had been the more shocking to her caller; the description of her cosy little romantic affair in such terms, or the fact that a vicar would put it like that.

"For just over three years." The voice was a whisper now.

Rosemary thought back over the past three years, all the special occasions the family had shared together: birthdays, Christmases, anniversaries. And all the time, Joel had been... But who was she kidding. She'd known he was weak, even as she fell in love with him; and even after he started straying, while the kids were quite young and Rosemary herself was training for ordination, she'd carried on loving him.

But she was curious about one thing. "Why now? Why tell me now?" She paused as something occurred to her. "You're not the first, you know. And I'm sure you won't be the last. But you're the only one who's confessed to me." She was quite pleased with the liturgical reference; made her sound erudite while pointing out she was the injured party. She realised she was getting slightly hysterical.

"He dumped me." There was a bout of smoker's cough, and when she carried on speaking it sounded as though she was trying not to cry. "We always met on a Wednesday afternoon and evening." Too much information there, to Rosemary's mind. "But last week, he phoned and said he couldn't make it and we had to cool things. Something about being blackmailed."

"Oh, I find that hard to believe. Are you sure he wasn't just looking for an excuse to end the affair?"

"To be honest," and that wasn't a phrase Rosemary expected to hear from this woman's mouth, "that's what I thought. He said it wasn't an end, just a pause. But I'd reconciled myself to losing him, and had started to move on." Rosemary wondered if it was her role as a vicar that made this woman think she could talk to her like this. Although there was a good chance Joel hadn't told her what his wife did. "Then yesterday, he phoned again, full of the joys of spring, expecting me to drop everything and make myself available as soon as he called. So I told him I was busy and put the phone down on him."

"This is all very interesting," Rosemary wondered if the woman would recognise the irony in her voice, "but you still haven't told me why you're calling me. Surely you're not expecting me to give you my blessing to continue this affair with my husband?"

"Oh no, the affair is very definitely finished. I won't stay with a man who mucks me about like that."

"Very commendable, a woman with integrity." Rosemary had now moved from irony to sarcasm. "So this is a revenge call? You're miserable, so you're making sure both Joel and I are too?"

"Not at all. To be honest," there it was again, that phrase, "I toyed with the idea of ringing the police instead. But I thought I would talk to you first."

"Why the police? Adultery may be against God's law, but I don't think it's something the Devon and Cornwall Police would be interested in."

"Not adultery, no. But how about murder?" There was a silence and then a chuckle at the other end of the line. "Yes, I thought that would grab your attention."

Rosemary felt a cold breeze blow over her. "Murder? Whose murder?"

"I believe there was a death in your village over the weekend? An elderly woman found in a swimming pool. I heard the news report, the police suspect foul play and are looking for witnesses."

"And how does this have anything to do with my husband? You're surely not suggesting…"

"I'm not suggesting anything, Reverend," so Joel had

told her he was married to a vicar, "all I'm doing is reporting the facts as I see them. Last week, Joel told me he was being blackmailed, and we had to cool it. Yesterday he told me he knew who the blackmailer was, and that we no longer had anything to worry about, because she was dead."

Rosemary felt the hysteria rising in her once more, and this time she let go of it, laughing briefly before taking a deep breath. "Well, that's the best story I've heard all week. The idea of my Joel being a murderer is just as laughable as the idea of Josephine Hillson being a blackmailer. Don't bother to call again. Good day to you."

Her mood was totally destroyed, and Rosemary knew she would get no more work done on her sermon that day. As she collected her notes together and walked back towards the vicarage, she couldn't get the woman's voice, and the questions she had raised, out of her mind.

CHAPTER 22

Dylan Foster threw down the chisel and mallet with a cry of frustration. He stared at the piece of tree trunk he was trying to turn into a realistic-looking owl, and accepted it wasn't going to happen. Not with that piece of wood anyway. And not with the mood he was in that day. He stared out of the shelter he'd built for himself, high up on Dartmoor. On a clear day he could see Plymouth, or at least the sea. But today it was cloudy and he could barely see a few hundred metres across the moors.

A bit like his mind, he realised. Liked a good metaphor, did Dylan. He made a note of that one in the hand-stitched, leather-bound notebook he'd bought off a market stall at the Totnes Christmas Market. Maybe he could use it in one of his poems. Although he wasn't going to be writing any poetry today either, he suspected.

How could he have been so stupid? He'd trusted Hilly. She'd been a guiding force during a bad time in his childhood and they'd remained friends ever since. Or so he'd thought. Which was why, when he got the first letter saying his secret was out, she was the one he turned to, rather than his mother.

The letter had arrived with a pile of bills and other junk mail a few weeks previously, and he'd thrown it on the counter in the kitchen. It wasn't until he received a reminder from his mother to pay the Council Tax bill that he'd gone searching through the pile of papers and found the expensive-looking cream envelope with the green writing. It had been stamped, but the postmark was indistinct and he couldn't make it out. And he must have thrown the envelope out at some point, because he no longer knew where it was.

But the letter was different. The letter sat inside his notebook, burning a hole in his pocket and screaming out to him even when he wasn't looking at it. He'd taken it out and read it numerous times, trying to decide what to do. There was nothing specific; the wording just said: *I know what you did and it's time you paid for your sins.* Which left it all up to his imagination. And one thing Dylan had was a vivid imagination.

What sins could it be referring to? He was fairly certain they weren't talking about his current life. He was a non-smoking, non-drinking vegan who cycled everywhere he could and always took public transport if possible, rather than driving. In fact, he didn't even have a driving licence. He was his own boss, employed no-one, and made his money on a variety of activities, including the wood carving he'd just abandoned in despair. He'd tried various money-making schemes in the past, some with more success than others, but he'd only ever cheated the tax man; never a fellow human being. Okay, so he had a trust fund from his father and lived in the basement of his mother's house, but he couldn't help it if his parents were rich – and he used their money as little as possible.

No, Dylan, was pretty sure it was his past the letter was referring to, rather than his present. And that could only mean one thing. His brother. Dougal. Older than Dylan by half an hour, Dougal had been his *bête noire* since long before either of them knew the term. Unusually for twins, they had never bonded and were more likely to be found fighting than enjoying each other's company as they grew up.

And even Dougal's death in a drowning accident at the age of seven hadn't released Dylan from his brother's shadow. If anything, it had made things worse. When his parents' marriage ended soon afterwards the young Dylan was convinced it was his fault, and even in his thirties, despite logic telling him he was wrong, he still felt he needed to prove himself to his mother and to anyone who'd known the twins as children.

The only person who he didn't need to prove himself to was Josephine Hillson. Hilly had been a friend of his mother, and Arabella had employed her to look after the grieving young boy. He'd not realised it at the time, but Arabella had been fighting her own battles and had been unable to look at her remaining son without seeing his double.

Hilly was a no-nonsense companion – they all agreed he was too old for a nanny – who had been in the wars herself. When she arrived, she was limping, and said she'd been in a car crash. But she wasn't prepared to talk about it – or about Dougal's death and the aftermath. She insisted on setting up a home-schooling curriculum for Dylan, and right from day one, never allowed him to feel sorry for himself. She set him homework which he was expected to deliver on time each day. But so long as he complied with her rules, she could be a wonderful friend who took him out and about in the countryside. He remembered she was an avid scrapbook keeper, and he'd helped her collect flowers, leaves and other small souvenirs of their days out.

So, when the letter finally got too much for him to bear on his own, it was to Hilly he'd turned. She'd listened to everything he'd said and while not giving her opinion, had asked pertinent questions which had helped him decide what to do.

It was only when the second letter arrived, the day after their meeting, feeding back to him some of his own words and pointing out why ignoring the problem was not going to work, that Dylan realised Hilly had turned out not to have been his friend after all.

She'd betrayed him, blackmailed him and must have been laughing at him the whole time he'd been telling her his tale of woe. And now Josephine Hillson was dead. And Dylan Foster wasn't sorry at all.

CHAPTER 23
SATURDAY 7TH SEPTEMBER

The phone rang as Cath Wootton was changing the bedclothes in the master bedroom. She tucked the phone between her ear and her shoulder, as she carried the bundle of dirty sheets downstairs.

"Hello? Cath speaking."

"Hi there, it's only me." Cath recognised her sister-in-law's voice. "Not disturbing you, am I?"

"On the contrary, Sal, I'm always happy to be interrupted when I'm doing the laundry. You know how I hate wash day."

Sal laughed. "Not your favourite job, is it, changing the beds?" She paused. "I'm going into The Willows later and wondered if you needed anything from M&S?"

Now that didn't sound like Sal at all. She hated shopping in the way Cath hated changing beds. And she particularly hated department stores, which she always said were overcrowded and overpriced. Cath wondered what her sister-in-law was really calling for. No doubt the true reason would come out fairly soon.

"Not today, thanks, love. I've got a Tesco delivery coming later on and we're having takeaway tonight. My reward for getting the washing done while Mervyn's at work."

"On the early shift, is he?"

"Right. Finishes around three. Should be home before five."

"Did you hear the local news this lunchtime?" Ah, so now they were getting to it. "Police have confirmed that the body found in the swimming pool in Coombesford was definitely Josephine Hillson and she was definitely murdered."

"Oh, Sal, that's dreadful. No, I missed that."

"Does Mervyn know?"

"Shouldn't think so. He'd have told me."

"Unless he's got something to hide, that is."

"Now just a minute, Sal, what are you suggesting?"

"Only that Mervyn was upset at meeting first Josephine Hillson and then that niece of hers. I just wondered if maybe he'd taken things too far."

"Absolutely not. My Mervyn's not like that. He'd never do anything violent."

Cath had dropped the pile of bedding on the floor and was sitting on the bottom of the stairs. She heard Sal give a deep sigh and the next words seemed to be dragged out of her. "Except we both know that's not true, don't we, Cath? Mervyn could be very violent back in his BNP days."

"Thirty years ago, maybe, but he's a changed person. Has been ever since Sean first brought you home and introduced you as his future wife. My Mervyn changed when he realised he was in danger of losing his brother. He left the BNP and all that right-wing fascist nonsense behind him. In fact, I happen to know he deeply regrets ever getting involved with them."

"Hmm, maybe. I do hope you're right."

A sudden thought occurred to Cath. "When did you say they found the body?"

"Sunday night. Apparently there was some sort of village fete going on and no-one realised she was missing until the end of the evening. Police think she was killed some time around nine."

"Well, there you are then. How could Mervyn have been involved?" She couldn't believe she was even having this conversation, but carried on anyway. "He was with you from mid-afternoon and he was back here by nine-thirty."

"No, he wasn't with me."

"But I thought he was doing that bit of plumbing you'd asked him to look at. That's what he said…"

"I'm sorry, Cath, I was out from around lunchtime on Sunday. An old school-friend of mine was down from Swansea for a few days and we had lunch together. Then afterwards, I went for a long walk on the coastal path. Didn't get home until after nine."

"And Mervyn didn't do the work while you were out?"

"How could he? He doesn't have a spare key since we got the new locks installed. I was going to get one cut today while I was out shopping."

Cath stood up and gathered up the sheets. She hoped her voice sounded brisk to her sister-in-law. "Well, I must have misunderstood him. I'll ask him when he gets back tonight. But one thing I do know, Sal, is that my Mervyn is no killer." She made a point of banging the door of the washing machine open. "Right, can't stop any longer. This washing isn't going to do itself. Bye, Sal." And with a decisive click, she disconnected the call.

Later, while she was putting the clean sheets and pillowcases on the bed and stuffing the quilt into a matching cover, her mind churned with the conversation she'd just had. She and Sal had always got on well, and since Sean was killed, the two families had spent more time together than apart.

But how dare she. How dare she suggest that Mervyn might be responsible for the death of Josephine Hillson. Yes, he'd been upset when she'd accosted him in his workplace. And even more so when he'd bumped into Veronica Penfold. And Sal was certainly right when she alluded to Mervyn's bad-boy days in the BNP. But that was a different time, a different man. How could Sal even think that he'd be involved in murder?

But where had he been on Sunday afternoon? And why had he lied to her? They had a good marriage. Like most couples, they'd had their ups and downs. But they never lied to each other. Until now. And she had to admit Sal was right. If Mervyn hadn't been at his sister-in-law's house sorting out a leaking tap, just where had he been? She'd definitely be asking him that as soon as he arrived home.

Then a sudden thought struck her so hard she had to sit down to catch her breath. Mervyn had no alibi for the time of the murder – not that he was going to need one, she told herself – but by the sound of it, neither did Sal. And if there was one person who had more cause to hate Josephine Hillson than the brother of the man she'd killed in a car crash, it was that man's wife, who'd been left a widow with a young family to bring up on her own.

Maybe there was another reason why Sal was so eager to point the finger at her brother-in-law.

CHAPTER 24

"Someone's looking very thoughtful."

Olga's voice broke into Rosemary's reverie, and she looked up, trying to pin a smile on her face. It was the wrap-up meeting for the Summer Social committee, now reduced to the two of them, and they'd agreed to meet in the vicarage garden.

"Just thinking about my life and the future." Rosemary realised that sounded really profound and laughed nervously, to try to deter any further enquiry from her friend and neighbour.

But Olga, for all her frivolous appearance and youthful dress sense, had a wise head on her shoulders. "That does sound serious. Anything I can do to help?"

"Isn't that supposed to be my line?"

"Everyone needs someone to talk to occasionally. So take off the dog collar for a moment and tell Auntie Olga all about it."

Rosemary stared at Olga in silence for a while then came to a decision. "You're right. I could do with a friendly listening ear." She stood up and pointed towards the house. "But this could take a while, so I'm going to get the coffee first."

Within minutes, she was back and the two women

nibbled on Celia Richardson's chocolate chip cookies and sipped their coffee in companionable silence.

Olga put down her cup, wiped the crumbs from her fingers with a paper napkin and nodded to Rosemary. "Okay, shoot. What's the problem?"

"It's difficult to know where to start." Rosemary bit her lip. "It could start with Joel. Or then it could start with poor dear Josephine, God rest her soul." Olga glanced up heavenward while Rosemary stared straight ahead. "But for me it started with a phone call I received yesterday."

"Well start there and see where it takes us."

"I had a call from someone who told me she and Joel had been 'seeing each other' as she so delicately put it."

Olga held up a hand in dramatic fashion. "Hold on. Are you saying your Joel…? Surely not? You guys are so good together."

Rosemary wondered if Olga was protesting just a tad too much, but remembered the Ukrainian woman had only been in the village for a few years and had only really started integrating with the community since she became a widow five years previously. There was no reason why she should know about Joel's tendency to go after every attractive woman in sight. Although come to think of it…

"That's very kind of you, Olga, but you must know Joel has a wandering eye – and sometimes more than that. Do you mean to tell me he's never tried to hit on you?"

"Poof." Olga waved a hand dismissively. "Sure, he tried, but then most men do." She seemed to have no awareness of how that last statement sounded and Rosemary hid a smile as Olga went on, "I slapped him down and he never tried it again." She rested her hand briefly on Rosemary's arm. "But I really had no idea he would ever be unfaithful to you. It must have come as a terrible shock."

Rosemary shrugged. "Not really. I've known for years. It started when I was training for the Ministry. But he always comes back to me once he gets bored and so long as it didn't impact on the rest of us, I just let him get on with it." She pulled a face. "It's not as though I can divorce him, after all."

"So why the call?"

"She reckons he dumped her last week following the receipt of a blackmail letter."

Olga sat up straight. "Did you say blackmail letter?"

"That's right. Apparently someone wrote to him saying–"

"I know what you've been doing and I know who with?"

"Sounds about right." Rosemary put her head on one side and stared at Olga, a suspicion forming in her head. "Why? How did you know?"

"Because I got one too." Olga raised one beautifully outlined eyebrow. "And before you ask, no, I am not Joel's other woman."

Rosemary felt a pang of guilt. She'd spoken to the other woman: she was a heavy smoker with a cut-glass English accent. Olga was anything but. "Never crossed my mind." She wondered when she'd learned to lie so easily. "What did you do about it?"

"Them, not it. I got three altogether. I threw them in the bin, darling. I have nothing to hide, so there's nothing to fear from a malicious act like that." She put on a mock sad face. "I've been as pure as a nun ever since Simon was killed." Then she grinned. "Although not for the want of trying, I must admit."

Rosemary chuckled along with her friend. Then she cleared her throat. "Actually, the news about the affair, or even about the blackmail, wasn't the worst part of the call."

"Really?"

"According to my caller, Joel changed his mind earlier this week. Tried to get back with her again. He reckoned he'd found out who the blackmailer was but they no longer had anything to fear."

"Don't tell me he'd paid them off."

"Nope. He told her the blackmailer was dead."

"Well how on earth could he possibly have known that?"

"Because he claimed the blackmailer was Josephine."

"Josephine who? I only know one…" Olga stopped speaking and her eyes widened as she appeared to realise the implications of what Rosemary had just said. "No. I don't believe it. Josephine Hillson was a blackmailer? That's ridiculous."

"That's what I said. But the caller swore it was true. She said Joel had worked it out. And when he called her a second time, he was very upbeat and said they had nothing more to worry about, as the old woman was dead."

"Well, even if it was true, and I'm still having a hard time accepting that sweet old lady was a blackmailer…" Rosemary wasn't sure she would have described the late lamented former schoolteacher as sweet but decided to let it go. "Why call you in that way? Wouldn't it be in her interests to make sure you didn't know?"

"Oh, she'd already decided to end the affair anyway." Rosemary paused and thought hard before putting her final thoughts into words. Once out there, they couldn't be taken back. "She suspected Joel had something to do with Josephine's murder and wanted me to know she was considering talking to the police."

Olga burst into peals of laughter at that point. "Oh, sweetie, is that what's been worrying you? For goodness sake, if the idea of Josephine Hillson being a blackmailer is difficult to swallow, the thought of your Joel being a murderer is even more insane."

CHAPTER 25
SUNDAY 8TH SEPTEMBER

In the event, it wasn't until the following day that Cath had a chance to talk to Mervyn. He'd arrived home on the Saturday evening with a raging headache brought on, he claimed, by a day of horrendous traffic and snarled-up roadworks. He'd grabbed a quick cup of tea and headed straight for bed. By the time Cath had eaten her solitary takeaway, cleared up the kitchen and was ready to join him, he was fast asleep in the freshly laundered bedclothes and didn't even stir when she climbed in beside him.

By the next morning he was his old self again, and suggested they went out for a meal that night. Cath readily agreed. Mid-evening, full of steak and chips, they sat on a bench overlooking Torquay harbour enjoying a post-prandial cigarette (Mervyn) and ice-cream cone (Cath).

"I had a call from Sal yesterday." Cath tried to keep her voice calm, although she could hear the nerves behind her statement. Just where would this conversation lead?

"Yeah? Everything okay with her, was it?"

"Well, she still needs that tap mending." Cath felt rather than saw Mervyn go very still. She looked at him with raised eyebrows, but he said nothing. "But that wasn't why she called." She waited, but there was still no reply. "She rang to tell me about Josephine Hillson's murder."

"Oh."

"Yes, oh." Cath turned towards her husband and grabbed his hand. "Why didn't you mention it to me? You must have known."

Mervyn nodded. "Yes, I knew. I heard about it. I didn't want to upset you."

"Why would it upset me? I've never met the woman. I only ever saw her from a distance during the inquest."

Mervyn shook his head. "I can't explain, Cath. Let's just say I had my reasons and leave it at that."

"No, I don't think so. I need to know why you didn't mention the death of a woman who played a major part in your life. And I also need to know why you lied to me about where you were last Sunday." She crossed her arms and glared at him, while he stared down at his feet. "I'm waiting, Mervyn."

As she watched her husband of more than a quarter of a century, a man she'd always looked up to and respected as well as loving deeply, he began to shrivel before her eyes. It was as though a pin had pricked him and he shrank in on himself. Finally he looked up and nodded at her.

"You're right, Cath, as always. I shouldn't keep secrets from you." He rubbed his forehead as though marshalling his thoughts. Then he sat up straight.

"I didn't go to see Sal on Sunday. That had been my original intention, but on the Saturday, she phoned me to say she was going out for lunch with a friend." He smiled sadly. "I was going to take you out to lunch, but on the way home that afternoon, I saw a poster for the Summer Social in Coombesford and realised that would be an opportunity for me to meet up with Miss Hillson without having to try and find her address."

"Sorry. You went to Coombesford on Sunday?" Mervyn nodded, biting his lip. "But why? I thought after you saw her that time in Exeter, you said you didn't want to see her ever again."

"I know what I said. But I've had time to think things through since then. One of the things she said to me that day was that she wanted to make some sort of restitution for Sean's death." He sighed. "At the time, I was so angry with her, I told her we wanted nothing to do with her or her money."

"Oh, Mervyn…"

"Yes, I know. Later I realised I'd been hasty and shouldn't be speaking for Sal and the family. Now the kids are grown up, setting up homes, starting families, the sort of help they might have expected if Sean had still been with us isn't available from Sal on her own."

"And although you always try to do your bit…"

"Precisely. We have our own kids to look after." He put his hands on his hips and flexed back his shoulders, breathing deeply. "So I decided I would see if I could persuade Miss Hillson I'd been wrong. Maybe see if she could find a way of giving Sal some support."

"And did you see her?"

"I did, yes. Apparently she was on the organising committee for that fundraising day, so she was very busy, but I caught her at an opportune moment and we grabbed a quick cup of tea."

"And did you manage to persuade her?"

"Didn't need to. Seems she'd decided to ignore my original reaction and had set up a trust fund in Sal's name, which could be called on at will, starting immediately. And in the event of her death," he swallowed hard, "most of her estate would be going to Sal as well."

"Oh, Mervyn, that's so generous of her." Cath stopped as a thought struck her. "But would Sal accept it?"

"Not for herself, no I don't think so. But like any mother, I think Sal would do anything for her kids."

"So Sal's a wealthy woman now? I guess she doesn't know yet?"

"Presumably not, or she'd have told us."

Cath bit her lip. She was delighted for her sister-in-law,

but there was something else niggling at her.

"What time did you leave Coombesford?"

"About six-thirty, I think. I popped into Newton Abbot to see a mate for a while and then came straight home to you. Why?"

"And you swear Miss Hillson was alive when you left?"

"Of course I do. What on earth? Oh, Cath, don't tell me you think…?"

"No, of course I don't. But Sal does. Or at least she was doing some pretty heavy finger-pointing when she phoned. And I wondered – I can't believe I'm saying this – but I wondered if she had a reason for casting the blame in your direction?" Mervyn stared at her with a look of horror on his face. "What? What is it, Mervyn?"

"She was there. On Sunday evening. I only caught a glimpse in the crowd, and I thought I was mistaken. But now I'm pretty certain, Cath. Sal was in Coombesford when Josephine Hillson was killed."

CHAPTER 26
MONDAY 9TH SEPTEMBER

"I'm just running across to have a word with Veronica about the wake. I won't be long." Esther popped her head around the door of the bar. Rohan, deep in conversation with one of the old-timers who spent many an hour sipping their beer and telling tales of their youth, nodded and winked at her. His companion didn't even pause for breath.

When Charlie and Annie had first asked them to run The Falls during the four weeks they'd planned for their honeymoon, Esther and Rohan had quickly agreed. And even when that honeymoon had been delayed, rescheduled and extended to six weeks, they were still happy to help out. Esther was quite enjoying working alongside Rohan day in, day out. But neither of them had expected to have to deal with another suspicious death in the village at the same time. Or more importantly, from Esther's point of view, a large wake to cater for.

Veronica had phoned The Falls that morning to say the police had released Josephine's body following the completion of the forensic post-mortem, and she was keen to lay her aunt to rest as soon as possible. A date had been set for two weeks' time. Could she use The Falls for the wake? She was sure many of Miss Hillson's former pupils would be keen to attend.

After a few moments of complete panic, Esther had said she'd get back to Veronica that afternoon. Then she'd phoned Celia, who'd phoned Olga, Melanie and everyone else with the slightest cooking ability, and between them, they'd come up with a plan. Now all Ester had to do was agree the details with Veronica.

As Esther left the car park and turned right towards the village green, she glanced up at the sky. The morning had started bright, clear and sunny, but now small wisps of white floated across the face of the sun and turned it hazy. The slight breeze was a touch chill and she shivered, wishing she'd slipped a jacket over her sleeveless top.

Nevertheless she revelled, as always, in the freedom of being able to wander around the village on her own. Free from the crippling anxiety attacks that had plagued her for so long, keeping her a virtual prisoner in her own home, Steele Farm. Her release had started two years before when she'd been forced outside by a fire that was threatening her father's life. Since then, with his help, and latterly with Rohan's as well, she'd gradually returned to a state of calm that allowed her to fully function as she wished. But she never took it for granted.

Josephine Hillson's cottage was located in the cul-de-sac just past the school and Cosy Café. Esther assumed Veronica would inherit it; as far as anyone knew, the two women had been very close and Josephine had no other family, apart from Veronica and her invalid mother. And if she did inherit it, would she move into the village to live, hire it out maybe as a holiday cottage, or put it up for sale?

Pushing open the gate and walking up the front path, Esther paused to admire the roses. They had been Josephine's pride and joy; many had been planted by her father, she'd frequently told people. Josephine had always kept up with her pruning, but now, quite a few of the blooms were past their best. Esther hoped Veronica was a keen gardener too. It would be sad to see the flowers suffering from neglect. She bent her head to smell one of the large blowsy blooms. Somehow the smell wasn't quite right today. Did flowers mourn for their lost gardeners?

Esther knocked on the front door. An upstairs window was open, and the lace curtain waved lazily in the breeze. But no sound came from inside the house. Esther knocked again. Still nothing. Glancing around, she noticed the haze was getting thicker. Were they in for a storm?

Maybe Veronica was in the back garden. Esther crossed the front of the cottage and walked around the corner to where a small garage was set back from the road. A faint humming sound came from inside and Esther shrieked as she realised the haze was not from clouds across the sun but from fumes billowing under the door.

"Help! Somebody help me!" she screamed, but looking back across at the green, she saw it was deserted. She raced to the garage and yanked open the door. Josephine's car was idling gently, almost hidden by fumes. A tube was attached to the exhaust and had been poked through an opening in the side window. To her horror, Esther saw someone in the driver's seat, slumped over the wheel. It was Veronica.

Praying the doors wouldn't be locked, Esther grabbed a handle and pulled hard. The door swung open and Veronica's body slumped sideways towards her. Esther leaned in and switched off the engine. Then, there was a moan, and Esther realised the other woman was still alive. Grabbing Veronica's shoulders, she tried to haul her out of the car, but for some reason she was unable to move her.

It was then she saw Veronica was a prisoner in the vehicle, her wrists enclosed in cable ties that were wound around the steering wheel. Esther swung around to the workbench running down the side of the garage and seized the secateurs that were hanging from a hook. Snapping the ties, she hauled Veronica out of the car, away from the garage and onto the lawn.

Pulling her phone from her pocket, she dialled the emergency services. "Ambulance, please." She hesitated.

"And police."

By the time the ambulance arrived, closely followed by a squad car, Veronica was beginning to stir. Esther gave her details to the police and told them where they'd find her when they were ready to take a statement. Then she left the professionals to their job and slowly walked away from the cottage that, for the second time in as many weeks, would be the centre of a police investigation.

She had no idea what had gone on in the two hours between Veronica phoning to book The Falls and Esther arriving to talk through the details. But what she did know was that, contrary to her initial thought, Veronica Penfold had not tried to kill herself. The cable ties twisted around her wrists, attaching her to the steering wheel, were a clear indication that someone else had been involved.

CHAPTER 27
TUESDAY 10TH SEPTEMBER

"She's still a bit sleepy, but she had a good night's rest and we're hoping to let her go home later today. I can let you have ten minutes with her."

The nurse's voice drifted across Veronica's drowsiness and warned her she was about to have a visitor. She reluctantly opened her eyes as DC Joanne Wellman entered carrying a large holdall that looked vaguely familiar. She thought she'd seen it in the cupboard under the stairs in Josephine's cottage.

"DC Wellman, how nice to see you." The two women had met when Veronica had returned to Coombesford following the news of her aunt's death. Veronica had found her to be pleasant, if a bit dim at times.

"How're you feeling, Ms Penfold?" The young detective pulled a chair towards the bed, its legs scraping across the floor and setting Veronica's teeth on edge. "It looks like you had a lucky escape. If Ms Steele hadn't arrived when she did…"

Veronica shuddered. "Please, I'd rather not think about it."

The DC nodded. "Yes, of course." She paused before continuing, "But I do need to ask you some questions if you feel up to it?" Veronica nodded and then wished she hadn't, as her head spun. "Do you have any idea who did this to you?"

"I'm afraid not. I went into the garage to get something and I was grabbed from behind, a cloth held over my nose and that was the last thing I remember until coming around in the ambulance."

"You don't remember being tied to the steering wheel, then?"

"No, nothing at all, I just told you." Really, how dim could this woman be? What part of nothing did she not understand?

"Okay, we'll leave that part of it for now. Can you think of anyone who might wish you harm? You're not from around here, are you? Do you have any enemies in this part of the world?"

Veronica yawned delicately behind her hand, hoping it would give the hint she was tiring. "I've been wracking my brains but can't come up with anyone around here – or anywhere else for that matter." She drummed her fingers on the bed covers as she pondered her next words very carefully. "I did wonder if it was somehow connected to my aunt, rather than to me. After all, we don't know why she was killed, do we?"

"And you have some thoughts on that, Ms Penfold?"

"Well, I'm waiting to hear from the solicitor, but I believe I'm the main beneficiary of Aunt Josephine's will. Money is a powerful motivator for some people, I understand."

"Forgive me, Ms Penfold, but your aunt was a retired schoolteacher who worked part time as a parish clerk. And yet her bank accounts show she had a considerable amount of savings. Did she have another source of income that we're not aware of?"

"Ah. Interesting you should mention that." Veronica looked across at the holdall. "Are those my things?"

"Yes. I've brought your handbag and a change of

clothes. I hope that was okay?"

"Very kind. Thank you. Could I have my handbag please?" She rummaged around and pulled out a small green book which she held tightly in her hand as she continued talking. "I found this in my aunt's study and was going to ring you about it, but I got waylaid." She raised her eyebrows, but DC Wellman didn't laugh. Not only dim, but with no sense of humour, then.

"What is it?"

"I think it may be the key to why my aunt was killed. Tell me, DC Wellman, in your investigations so far, did you find any suggestion that she might have been a blackmailer?"

This time, Joanne Wellman did laugh. "A blackmailer? You're joking, aren't you?"

"I can assure you, young lady, I would never joke about such a serious matter as my aunt's murder." There, that wiped the smile off the silly young woman's face. Veronica felt a frisson of satisfaction as she handed over the little green book, together with the part-finished letter she'd found in her aunt's bureau. "You've got experts on the force with more experience than me, but it looks like a list of names and amounts received. And it goes back a good few years. Certainly far enough to explain the excess savings."

DC Wellman flicked through the pages, pausing every so often to read some details before moving on. Veronica had studied the book thoroughly before deciding to hand it to the police. She knew each page contained dates, initials and amounts, all in the hundreds. Several of the initials appeared more than once over the years.

When she reached the final page, DC Wellman looked up. "These final initials are more recent. And they don't have any amounts against them. Do you have any idea what that might mean?"

Was she going to have to spoon-feed this woman? "I suspect it's a new group of targets. And before you ask, I have no idea who they might be. But maybe you could check with the Coombesford crowd. If these targets are local, they'll be able to tell you who they are." She had another thought. "And if they're not local, why not try her address book. You never know your luck. She might just have written a name and address in there that will help you on your way."

Veronica lay back against the pillows and hoped this detective would take the hint and leave her alone now. She'd handed over two pieces of incriminating evidence that pointed to her aunt being anything but the upright member of the community everyone thought her to be. So although she might well have provided the clues the police needed to make an arrest, she'd ruined Josephine Hillson's reputation in the process. Added to which, her head was aching and her wrists were sore from yesterday's misadventure.

All she wanted now was the peace and quiet to recover her health and mourn her loss.

CHAPTER 28

"Yes, Sarge, really. A blackmailer." Joanne Wellman handed the little green book and the sheet of notepaper to DS Derek Smith. "I had difficulty getting my head around it. But Veronica Penfold was adamant that's what's been going on." She shrugged. "To be honest, I wasn't surprised to hear the word. I was going to raise it myself. It was the link with Josephine Hillson I hadn't made."

"So who did you think it was?"

"Veronica Penfold. When I was getting her stuff ready to take to the hospital, I dropped her handbag upside down on the floor and a piece of paper fell out. It was that letter I've just given you. No envelope, so no idea who it was meant for. But as it was in Veronica's bag, I automatically assumed she was the writer.

"I put it back in her bag and was going to tackle her about it at the hospital. But she handed it over without any prompting and produced that little book at the same time. The deposits in Josephine's bank account agree with the amounts recorded, so it looks pretty conclusive."

"Fair enough." DS Smith handed the evidence back. "So where do you want to start?"

"From the latest names, I thought." Joanne pointed to the final page. "I've been through all the lists and most of the targets seem to appear more than once, which implies they prefer to pay for her silence. I thought maybe one of the new targets might have decided to take a different route."

"Possible. Of course one of the folks who's been paying up might have had too much. A case of the worm turning as it were."

"True, Sarge, but I still think we'll have more luck with the new targets – if we can identify who they are."

"Well, you make a start on that, while I see if I can get any clues on the older names." DS Smith walked back towards his desk, then stopped suddenly. "Hang on. What were those new initials again?"

"JL, OM and DF."

"Well, if I were you, I'd pop over to Coombesford and have a chat with the lady of the manor."

"What, Olga? Olga Mountjoy – of course."

"Yes, the delicious merry widow. If anyone's likely to make herself a target for blackmail, I suspect it would be her."

Olga Mountjoy was at home and happily led Joanne through the house and out onto the terrace, calling for Lindy to bring them a jug of something cool as they passed through the kitchen. She certainly didn't seem to Joanne like someone with something to hide. But then, killers had been known to be good actors in the past.

"So, what can I do to help the constabulary this fine morning?" The particularly English phrase sounded strange in Olga's Ukrainian accent.

"It's a rather delicate situation, I'm afraid, Ms Mountjoy."

"Sounds exciting." Olga rolled her eyes. "And for goodness sake, call me Olga."

"Well, Olga, I wonder if you've received any strange letters recently?"

Olga's mouth twitched and Joanne was sure there was a

knowing look in her eye. "Strange in what way?"

"Er, strange as in anonymous; threatening, even."

Now Olga laughed outright. "Oh, darling, if you could see your face. If you're referring to a letter attempting to blackmail me, then yes, I had one a couple of weeks back."

"Do you still have it?"

"I threw it straight in the bin. The only place for it. I've had them before and done exactly the same."

"You didn't think to report it to the police, then?"

"Why should I? It was just someone playing a prank. Probably kids, I would think."

"What did it say?"

"It said: I know what you've been doing; and I know who with. And before you ask the obvious question, no, I have nothing to hide. Which is why I didn't take it seriously."

"Well, okay, Olga. But can I just ask that if another letter arrives, you let me know straight away."

"Of course. Anything to help the police. You were so wonderful when my Simon…" Olga broke off and pressed her finger to her mouth momentarily. Then she seemed to give herself a mental shake. She sat up and looked shrewdly at Joanne. "But you're not expecting any more letters to arrive, are you, DC Wellman?"

"And why would that be, Olga?"

"It's pretty obvious, really. When a member of the Major Crime Investigation Team starts asking questions about blackmail attempts, it would imply the murder victim is suspected of being either one of the targets or the blackmailer themselves. And logically, it's more likely to be the latter." Olga giggled and then swapped her smile for an attempt at a serious face. "Which means you think Josephine Hillson was a blackmailer and that's probably what got her killed."

"I couldn't possibly comment, Olga." Joanne could feel herself going bright pink as the other woman arrived accurately at the right conclusion.

"Oh, darling, you don't have to." Olga waved a finger at her. "But all I can say is, you'll never be a decent poker player."

"Oh, what the hell." Joanne knew she was beaten and was glad DS Smith hadn't decided to make this visit with her. Although she suspected he would have found it no easier to dissemble with Olga than she had. "You're right. But please keep it to yourself, will you?" She paused, then came to a decision. "Look, let me ask you something. Do the initials JL mean anything to you?"

"In Coombesford, do you mean?" Olga shrugged. "Well, there's a woman that helps out in the post office. Janet I think her name is. Or Janice maybe. Yes, that's it, Janice Lemon. And one of the vicar's daughters is called Jacqueline, so that's Jacqueline Leafield." She clicked her fingers. "And of course, Rosemary's husband is called Joel Leafield, so I guess that's another one."

"And how about DF? Do you know anyone with those initials?"

Olga was silent, staring out over the garden, for a long time before looking up at Joanne. "No, I'm sorry, that doesn't mean anything to me."

And this time, Joanne got the feeling Olga was being completely honest. Whereas when she talked about the initials JL, there was a definite air of Olga having something to hide.

CHAPTER 29

It was twenty to three and the bar was empty when Olga popped her head around the door and waved at Rohan.

"Hi there, Olga. Do you want a drink?"

"No thanks. I'm just taking Bertie for a walk." A small white face appeared at her feet and a short bark confirmed the presence of the little Jack Russell, temporarily being spoiled at Mountjoy Manor until his family returned from Latin America. "I just wondered if you and Esther could call in on your way home tonight. There's something I need to talk to you about."

"Oh, I'm not sure, Olga. We're going to be pretty bushed by the time we leave here." He sighed. "I've no idea how Charlie and Annie keep going, day in, day out. We're only doing it for a few weeks and we're exhausted. Can't it wait?"

"Not really, no. It has to do with your investigation on behalf of the young Worcester boys."

Rohan felt a tinge of guilt. He'd promised Caroline he'd see what he could do about helping to clear her sons' names. But the days had just slipped by. He really needed to find some time to get on with it. "Fair enough, Olga, we'll be there. Tuesdays are normally quiet, so we should be able to get away pretty quickly."

In the event, there were no bookings for the restaurant that night, so Esther closed the kitchen early. Then Roger Richardson offered to take over running the bar and lock up for Rohan. It was just before nine when the pair rang the doorbell under the impressive portico of Mountjoy Manor.

Olga showed them into the sitting room. "I've been sitting out on the terrace for hours," she said, "but now the light's gone completely, it's a bit exposed and breezy out there."

Rohan took one end of the deep yellow sofa, while Olga curled herself up opposite him. Esther settled into the matching armchair, while Bertie flopped down on his bed in the corner. Rohan was amused to see Olga had managed to get one that matched the fabric of the soft furnishings exactly.

"Okay, Olga. We're here. What did you want to talk about?"

Olga pursed her lips, folded her arms and began. "Two weeks ago, I received a rather strange letter." She went on to tell Rohan and Esther about the contents of the letter and her reaction to it. "To be honest, I forgot about it almost as soon as I threw it away I'd had a couple of others months ago and just assumed someone was playing a joke on me. Then at the weekend, I had a long, rather disturbing talk with Rosemary." That tale took longer to tell and was interrupted several times as first Rohan and then Esther expressed disbelief about what they were being told.

"And to be honest, I shouldn't even be telling you about this. I promised Rosemary I'd keep it to myself."

"So what made you change your mind?" It was Esther who posed the question, but in doing so, she took the words right out of Rohan's mouth.

"I had a visit this morning from DC Joanne Wellman."

"And what did she want?" This time, it was Rohan who got there first.

"Well, she was pretty cagey to begin with, but she wanted to know if I'd received an anonymous letter. Apparently they found a list of initials among Josephine Hillson's papers and I was on the list. Or at least OM was, and they made an educated guess."

Esther was busy making notes on her tablet. "So it looks as though Rosemary's story about Josephine being a blackmailer is true, unlikely as it might sound."

Rohan laughed shortly. "Oh, believe me, I've come across a lot more unlikely stories. You never know what goes on behind closed doors – or in people's minds."

"In the end, I challenged DC Wellman and she caved in and admitted it. Terrible poker player, that girl would make." Olga grinned. "Then she asked me if I had any thoughts on two other sets of initials: JL and DF."

"JL. Joel Leafield." Esther bit her lip. "Oh no. Poor Rosemary."

"I know." Olga nodded. "I didn't want to cast suspicion on him, so prevaricated a bit, threw in a couple of other names, including Jackie Leafield, then acted as though I'd just remembered Joel's name. I feel terrible, but it would have been much more suspicious if I'd omitted his name altogether."

"Don't worry. Rosemary will understand." Rohan smiled sympathetically at Olga. "She's a vicar, for goodness sake. Honesty is part of her day job."

"Rohan's right, Olga. You can't blame yourself."

"Oh, I know that. I'll go and talk to her first thing in the morning. Hopefully warn her before the police get in touch." Olga sighed. "But it rather looks as though you need to add Joel to your suspect list, doesn't it?"

"Hmm." Rohan bit his lip. "I've not got a list as such, so far. Assuming we ignore Peter and Paul Worcester, there's Mervyn Wootton. And now there's Joel. That's it." He winked. "And I guess there's you, Olga." He held up his arms in surrender as both women protested loudly and Olga threw a cushion at him. "Sorry, only joking."

"What was the other set of initials?" Esther was tapping on her keyboard once more.

"DF. Why?"

"Well, I think I might know who that is. I was crossing the green a couple of weeks back and saw a young man leaving Miss Hillson's cottage. He gave her a big hug, before picking up a bike from the front garden and cycling away. She stood on the step waving to him until he was out of sight. It made such a nice picture, I asked her who he was. She told me he was someone she used to look after when she was younger. Seems she took a break from teaching for a while."

"Well, that's interesting." Rohan clicked his fingers. "Celia said something about that the other day."

"But the most interesting thing," Esther said, "was the young man's name. It was Dylan. Dylan Foster."

CHAPTER 30

"Is that you, love?" His mother's voice drifted down the stairs as Dylan hung his cycling helmet on the hook in the hallway and prepared to run down to the front door of his basement flat. He sighed. He'd almost made it. Maybe if he kept quiet, she'd think she'd misheard.

But no such luck. He heard a door opening and his mother's footsteps descending from the second floor. "I said, is that you, Dylan?"

"Well, if it isn't, your security isn't as good as you thought it was." He leaned across to kiss the top of her head as she drew level with him. "Hello, Ma. Good day?"

"Not bad. The council meeting was as boring as usual, but it was all over in less than an hour. Then I had lunch with the Simpsons in that new vegan place near the top of the hill. You must try it by the way. And then I went for a run to work off the calories from lunch."

"Calories from a vegan lunch? Surely not."

"Never heard of vegan wine?" She waggled her eyebrows at him. "And then I did a bit of shopping. Not long been home."

"Sounds busy." He was well used to his mother's packed schedule. And he knew the comment about the wine was a joke. Her sponsor would be devastated – and so would he

– if his mother fell off the wagon after so many years.

Arabella Prescott had reverted to her maiden name when she'd left Dylan's father. But the couple had remained friends until the day Reginald Foster died, and he left her his considerable business assets to add to the settlement she'd had following the divorce. So bringing up a son on her own had never been a financial hardship. She was a town councillor, a leading light in several local charities, not to mention a stalwart member of the local WI. She was the most important person in Dylan's life, while at the same time, she could be the most irritating presence on his shoulder.

"Are you going out tonight?" She asked him the same question every time she saw him, no doubt hoping he would go and find himself a nice girl – or maybe boy – to hook up with.

And as usual, his response was the same. "Not tonight, no. I thought I'd have a quiet night in."

"Want to eat with me, then?"

"Maybe later. I need a shower first."

"Well, you know where I am when you're ready." With a wave of her hand she set off back up the stairs. Then she stopped and hit her forehead with her palm. "I almost forgot. You had a call a while back. From the police."

His stomach hit the floor. "The police?"

"Yes, darling, you know. Those nice people in navy uniforms and pointy hats who used to be available if you needed to know the time when you were a kid."

"What did they want?"

"Didn't say. It was a young woman. She did give me her name, but I forget. It's written down somewhere. I'll find it later. Left a number, too. Asked if you could call her."

"But why did they call here?"

"I think they wanted to check you lived here. The phone's in my name, of course, so they weren't sure. But they said they'd been given this address for you." She pointed at him. "Been up to no good, have we?"

He shrugged. "Not as far as I know. If you find the bit of paper, I'll ring them later."

"Okay, poppet. See you in a while."

Dylan continued his delayed journey to his front door. By the time he'd found his key, let himself in and closed the door behind him, he could barely stand, he was trembling so much.

Surely Hilly hadn't had time to carry out her threat before she died? In her last letter, she'd threatened to report him to the police if he didn't start paying up regularly. She'd not signed the letter, of course. But he'd known it was her.

And he'd gone to talk to her in Coombesford, on the Saturday, the day before the Summer Social. The day before she'd been killed. She'd seemed shocked that he'd worked out who the letters had come from. But he'd seen no regret or sorrow in her gaze.

"Why now?" He'd caught her arm as she tried to walk away from him. "I was seven. You've known all these years. Why do this now?"

"Simple economics, dear boy. You've just turned thirty. No-one has any say over how you spend your trust fund any longer." And she'd pulled her arm free and turned on her heel without a backward look.

Had she accepted that he wasn't going to pay up and told the police out of spite? Or had she left a letter with her solicitor to be delivered to the police in the event of her death? What had she done? What had he done?

A sudden hammering on the door startled him and he gasped for air.

"Dylan, are you in there? I've found that paper with the DC's name and phone number. Dylan, can you hear me?"

Taking a deep breath and pinning a grin on his face, he opened the door.

"What were you doing in there? I've been knocking and calling for ages."

"I told you, Ma. I was about to have a shower." Calm. He had to keep calm or Arabella would suspect something.

But a good mother always knows when there's something not right with her child. And Arabella Prescott was a very good mother indeed. As she stared at him, he felt his face crumple.

"My poor boy. What on earth's the matter?" She opened her arms wide, and the thirty-year-old man reverted to the seven-year-old boy and sought comfort and refuge in his mother's embrace.

CHAPTER 31
WEDNESDAY 11TH SEPTEMBER

The house was an end-of-terrace a couple of roads back from the sea front. It was spotless and surrounded by a well-maintained garden overflowing with hydrangeas and bush fuchsias. Not the sort of residence one would necessarily associate with a member of the British National Party. Nor, for that matter, was the woman of Caribbean heritage who answered the door.

When Esther had phoned to set up a meeting for Rohan with Mervyn Wootton, he'd been at work and she'd spoken instead to his wife. Cath Wootton had been pleasant and understood exactly why they wanted to talk to her husband. But she was quite firm in saying that she'd much rather Rohan came and talked to her instead. "My husband's under a lot of stress at the moment and I won't have him upset unnecessarily." And when she pointed out politely that Rohan might be a former police officer and now a private detective, but that no-one was obliged to speak to him, Esther had given in.

And then Rohan had suggested Esther should go, rather than him. "You'll get more out of her, woman to woman." Esther wasn't so sure about that, but she'd agreed to give it a try. However, as she stood on that sunny doorstep, looking at the serious-looking woman in front of her, she began to have doubts once again.

"Mrs Wootton, I'm Esther Steele. We spoke on the phone."

The other woman's stern features melted into a huge smile. "Oh, I'm not Mrs Wootton, love. Well, actually I am in a way, but not the one you mean." Esther must have looked as confused as she felt. "Sorry, let's start again. I'm Sal, Mervyn's sister-in-law. Cath's just popped down to the shop for some biscuits. She'll be back in a minute. Come on in."

She led the way through an immaculate hall and kitchen, into a sunny conservatory and pointed to one of three easy chairs in a semi-circle around a coffee table. "Sit yourself down, Esther, did you say your name was? I thought your boss was coming. Or is he your husband?"

"Oh, he's not my husband." Esther felt herself blushing. "Nor my boss for that matter. In fact I'm his landlady." Then she realised that was irrelevant and shook her head. "I mean, we work together on cases occasionally."

"Whatever you say, love." Sal grinned at her. "Cath asked me to be here this morning. Said you were asking questions about Mervyn's past?"

"That's right. But shouldn't we wait until Mrs Wootton, I mean the other Mrs Wootton, gets back?"

"Oh, she'll be here soon. I rather suspect she's giving us a few minutes on our own first. So why don't you tell me what this is all about and why you want to drag up ancient history?" Sal's face had lost some of its friendliness.

Esther wondered how much Cath had told Sal, and decided to start from the beginning. "I don't know whether you saw on the local news the story about an elderly woman who was found dead in Coombesford a week or so back?"

"Josephine Hillson, you mean?"

"Right. Well, she was—"

"I know who she was. She was the woman who killed my husband." As a conversation stopper, it was right up there.

"Oh." Esther's mind went completely blank. "I don't know what to say. I'm sorry."

Sal shook her head. "No, it's me who should be sorry. I shouldn't have sprung it on you like that. And it was all a long time ago." She patted Esther's hand. "Carry on with what you were saying."

"Okay." Esther took a deep breath. "Miss Hillson had a niece, Veronica. She's staying in the village at the moment and she mentioned Mr Wootton to Rohan. Said there was something in the past that… oh…" Her voice faded away as she realised exactly what it was Veronica had been hinting at.

Sal said nothing, but the strange look on her face told Esther she too was thinking along the same lines. And Esther suddenly remembered exactly where Veronica was at the moment, and what had happened to her in the past few days. Had she been rash coming to meet this stranger, these strangers in fact, on her own?

At that moment, the front door slammed shut. "I'm home, Sal. Where are you?"

"Out the back, Cath." Sal rose and went to meet her sister-in-law. Esther could hear them conversing in a low tone in the kitchen, but was unable to make out any of the words. She reached in her pocket and pulled out her phone. Should she call Rohan? But if she did, he'd be too far away to get there in time. And if she was overreacting, she'd be worrying him unnecessarily.

"Here we are. A nice cup of tea." A small thin woman with blonde curly hair bustled into the conservatory, carrying a tray with three mugs, a teapot, milk jug and a plate of ginger biscuits and fig rolls. "Not much of a selection in the corner shop, I'm afraid." She wiped her hand down the side of her trousers and held it out towards Esther. "Miss Steele, I'm sorry I wasn't here to greet you. But hopefully Sal's been keeping you company."

Cath Wootton kept up a continual flow of chat as she

dispensed the tea, proffered biscuits, and apologised again for not being there when Esther arrived. She didn't question why Esther was there at all, rather than Rohan; presumably her sister-in-law had brought her up to speed on that.

Finally, her hostess settled herself in the third chair, took a deep drink from her mug and smacked her lips in appreciation. Esther felt herself beginning to relax once more. Which was rather unfortunate, since at that moment both Cath and Sal turned to stare at her. And neither had a trace of a smile left on their face.

"Okay, Miss Steele, Esther," Cath pointed at her, "I think it's time you told us exactly what this is all about and what it has to do with my Mervyn."

CHAPTER 32

"Hello, can I help you?" The bell had rung as Rosemary was just getting ready to visit a parishioner, and she was balancing a pile of books and her little briefcase as she opened the door. "Oh, hello, Joanne. Nice to see you. I won't shake hands if that's okay?" She thought back to her diary which she'd checked a few minutes before. "We don't have a meeting fixed for this morning, do we?"

DC Wellman shook her head. "No, you're okay, Rosemary. It's not you I've come to see today." The pair had occasional get-togethers to discuss their mutual support for a local kids' charity. "It's Joel I was hoping to talk to. Is he around?"

The words were innocent enough and the talk could have been about anything, but Rosemary went cold as she pondered the implications. Was this about Josephine Hillson? Did the police think Joel was involved in her death? And more to the point, was Joel actually involved in Josephine's murder?

"Rosemary? Did you hear me? I asked if Joel was about."

Rosemary started. "Sorry, Joanne, I was miles away. Yes, he's out in the back garden. About to cut the grass, I believe. Come on, I'll take you round there."

"You don't need to if you're busy." Joanne pointed to

the books in Rosemary's arms.

"It's fine. I'm heading for the back gate anyway. I'm just popping over to see one of my parishioners in the lanes. She can't get out as much as she used to and I always pick up her library books for her. Although," holding up one of the books, on the cover of which a young woman in white was being terrorised by a tall man with pointed canine teeth and a long black cape, "how she sleeps at night, reading this sort of stuff, I'll never understand."

The two walked in companionable silence around the side of the rectory. At least Joanne's silence appeared to be companionable. Rosemary's was teeming with indecision and the faint trace of panic. As they crossed the flat expanse of green and approached a small shed, the sound of banging and muttering could be heard.

Suddenly the muttering became a lot louder. "Damn thing! I'm going to scrap you and get a newer model!"

The two women exchanged amused looks. "He always struggles getting it started. But it's a great little mower really, and he wouldn't be parted from it." Rosemary raised her voice. "Joel, someone to see you."

As her husband came out of the shed, Rosemary reflected once again on how much the two of them had been through over the years, and how despite everything, she still loved him. Or at least, she did for now.

"What? Did you call? Oh, hello, DC Wellman. What can I do for you? Not in trouble, am I?"

His humour seemed heavy-handed and forced to Rosemary. She hoped that was just because she knew him well.

"I wanted a quick word, if that's okay, Mr Leafield." Joanne Wellman looked a trifle embarrassed as she glanced at Rosemary. "In private if that's possible."

"Oh, Rosemary and I have no secrets from each other, do we, darling?" Rosemary caught her breath at the sheer effrontery of that remark. She might have no secrets from him, but the reverse was definitely not so. As far as he knew anyway. And if she was honest, she was keeping the call from his mistress secret from him too.

"Sorry, Joel. I can't stop. I've got a busy round of calls this morning." She pinned a teasing smile on her face. "So whatever you've been up to, you're on your own, I'm afraid." And with a wave, she carried on towards the back gate and into the lane. Once through, she glanced back. Joel was staring after her with a forlorn look on his face.

Rosemary didn't see Joel again until early evening. The girls had gone to the theatre in Exeter and weren't expected back until late, so there were just the two of them for supper. Joel had offered to prepare it and called her from her study when it was ready.

"I've put our drinks out on the patio," he said. "Might as well enjoy the good weather while it lasts."

Once they were settled, he turned to her, the same forlorn look on his face. "I need your help, Rosemary." She said nothing, knowing there was more to come, and feeling disinclined to help him out in any way. "That visit from DC Wellman. You know she's part of the team investigating Josephine Hillson's death? Well, the police think I might be involved." He paused and took a deep breath. "I'm not, Rosemary. I swear I'm not. But I don't have an alibi for the time of the murder. And I need you to give me one."

Rosemary put down her drink. "Why don't you tell me all about it, Joel?"

The tale was rambling in places, which was probably because he was making it up as he went along. He didn't mention the 'other woman' but Rosemary guessed that was the last thing he wanted to talk about. Finally he ran out of words and stared helplessly at her.

"So let me get this straight, Joel. The police think you might have killed poor dear Josephine," actually, she'd have to stop thinking of her like that if she really was a blackmailer, "because she was trying to extort money from you about something she thought you were doing, but which you swear you weren't. But which you can't tell me about." He winced at the sound of her words, then nodded. "And you want me to give you an alibi?"

"Exactly. I knew you'd understand, Rosemary. And with your position in the community…"

"That's just it, isn't it, Joel?" She slammed her glass on the table and rose to her feet. "You want me, an ordained minister, to lie for you, because no-one's going to distrust a vicar. Yet you can't even do me the courtesy of being honest with me." She wasn't sure why she still didn't tell him she knew the whole background, but she didn't. "I'm sorry, Joel, but you really are on your own this time."

CHAPTER 33

After his breakdown the previous evening, Dylan had refused to talk to Arabella. But he had agreed to have supper with her the following evening, and he knew she wouldn't give up until she'd managed to get him to talk. Last time he'd confided in someone, it hadn't ended well. But Hilly had been a false friend. He knew that now.

His mother had been many things during his lifetime, but she'd never once let him down. Maybe he needed to trust her more. He spent part of the day scouting around the woods along the banks of the River Dart, looking for likely pieces of driftwood. But his heart wasn't in it and he spent more time sitting staring out across the water and planning what he was going to say.

By six-thirty he was home, showered and changed, and climbing the stairs to his mother's front door, a large bunch of garden flowers clutched in his hand. And he knew it didn't matter that it was her own garden he'd picked them from. It was the thought that counted. And that was exactly how Arabella took it.

"Michaelmas daisies, my favourite. Such a wonderful blue-purple colour. Pop them in a vase and put them on the end of the table so we can see them as we eat."

By tacit consent they chatted inconsequentially through

a vegan goats' cheese salad followed by courgette and mushroom ragu. It wasn't until they were sipping their coffee and nibbling on Arabella's home-made peanut butter and chocolate cookies that the mood turned serious.

Arabella put her cup down and cleared her throat. "Dylan, it breaks my heart to see you so unhappy. You know I love you and I'll support you whatever. But unless you tell me what's going on, how on earth can I help you?"

"I know, Ma." He linked his fingers together and squeezed hard. How was he going to get through this? Somehow he had to. "It's just hard."

"Well, let's start with the easiest bit. Did you ring DC Wellman back yet?"

"Not exactly."

"What does that mean? Either you did or you didn't."

"I didn't."

"Why not?"

"I looked her up. She's with the Major Crime Investigation Team in Exeter."

"So she probably wants to talk to you about Hilly. Although why you, rather than me? In fact, why either of us? We've not seen her for months." When Dylan didn't respond, Arabella looked sharply at him. "You know, don't you? You know what she wants to talk about."

"I think so, yes."

"And that's why you were so upset? Oh, Dylan, I know she was important to you at a difficult time of our lives, but shouldn't that make you more willing to help out, rather than less?"

"She wasn't as important as I thought." Dylan jumped up and began striding around the room. He tried to keep his tone even, but failed. "She was an old witch and I'm glad she's dead."

There was a shocked silence. Arabella picked up the jug and refilled their cups. Then she drank her coffee down in one go, eyeing him steadily over the rim of the cup. After a while, he sighed and sat down, pulling his own cup towards him.

"I saw Hilly in the week before she died. I got an anonymous letter that upset me and I didn't want to talk to you about it, so I went over to Coombesford and talked to her." Arabella opened her mouth as though to ask a question, then seemed to think better of it and closed it again. She nodded for him to continue.

Once Dylan started talking, it was suddenly a lot easier than he'd expected. He told Arabella about the contents of the letter, about the long conversation he'd had with Josephine Hillson, and the conclusion he'd come to that he was going to ignore it. He told her about the second letter that arrived soon after; and his realisation that Hilly was behind the blackmail attempt. And finally, he told her about the shocking argument he'd had with her on the day before she was killed. How she'd not only failed to defend herself against his accusations, but also sneered at him and threatened to expose him to the police."

"And now she's dead." His story told, he sat back and waited for Arabella to comment.

"But there's one thing I don't understand, Dylan. What on earth did Josephine," no longer Hilly, he noticed, "believe you'd done as a child that was worth blackmailing you for?"

He stared at her. Could she really not know? That time had been hard for all of them, but could she really not have worked it out? "I was there!" His voice rose to a screech and then broke. "The day Dougal drowned. We'd been fighting about something. I can't even remember what it was. But I was there right next to the stream and I did nothing to help him. He was my brother and I watched him die." His voice got quieter now as he laid out what he thought were the final pieces in the puzzle. "It gave me nightmares for years afterwards. One night while Hilly was looking after me, she overheard me talking in my sleep and worked it all out." He put his head on the table and sobbed gently, as he waited for his mother to condemn him as Hilly had done, and as he'd done himself, so long ago.

Arabella walked around to his side of the table and hugged him closely to her. "It wasn't you, darling. You didn't kill your brother. You have nothing to blame yourself for."

"But I could have reached him easily and pulled him out."

"And it would have made no difference at all. I'm so sorry, son. I should have realised you blamed yourself." Arabella took a deep breath. "Your brother had a congenital heart condition. He was dead before he hit the water. Dougal didn't drown and there was nothing you could have done about it."

Dylan froze in his mother's arms as the impact of her words hit him. It wasn't his fault. All these years he'd been blaming himself for nothing. And so had Hilly. "Oh my God, Hilly." He'd forgotten, for a moment, what had happened to Hilly.

CHAPTER 34

"And I have to say, for a moment or two I thought I was in trouble." Esther looked across at her companions with a smile that looked anything but confident. Rohan mentally kicked himself for sending her into danger. But before he could say a word, Esther held up her hand to stop him. "No more apologies, Rohan. I don't work for you. I work with you. And it was my decision to make the visit."

"Well said, Esther." The final member of the trio applauded. Olga had popped in for a drink after giving Bertie his final walk of the evening, and had happened to arrive at a quiet moment. With no-one else in need of a drink, and no bookings for the restaurant, Esther had taken the opportunity to tell them about her experience with the Wootton women earlier that day. "But you say they were fine once you explained why you were there?"

"Not fine, exactly, but I certainly didn't feel threatened by them. They were both very worried about Mervyn and keen to emphasise that he wouldn't hurt a fly."

Rohan pulled a face. "And did you believe them? Given his background?"

"I did actually, yes. It was Sal who mentioned it first. She asked me if I found it strange to see 'someone like her' as she put it, married into the Wootton family? She told me about first meeting the Wootton brothers at a party many years ago. Mèrvyn was there with a few of his BNP mates and they were giving her a hard time. But brother Sean stepped in and took her home. They got together, fell in love and decided to get married. And Sean gave Mervyn an ultimatum. Them or his mates. Either he sorted out his views and behaviour or he would lose his brother forever."

"And that worked?" Olga sounded a bit sceptical.

Esther nodded. "It did, yes. Apparently he wasn't that strongly into all that, he'd just got in with the wrong crowd and got led astray."

"Well, he was into it enough to get those tattoos." Now Rohan was sounding disbelieving. "And you know what they say about leopards and spots."

"True. But apparently, soon afterwards, Mervyn met Cath and she finished straightening him out. According to both women, he's regretted those tattoos ever since, and rarely wears short sleeves in public because of them. And they reckon he doesn't have a violent bone in his body."

"Hmm. It all sounds a bit convenient to me." Rohan turned to Olga. "Did Joanne Wellman mention Mervyn when she came to talk to you the other day?"

Olga shook her head. "Not at all. She seemed pretty focused on the blackmail targets." She clicked her fingers. "And she did mention the Worcester boys. Or at least I mentioned them in passing." She used her fingers to make speech marks around the words in the air. "She said they were still being treated as material witnesses rather than suspects, but she did say 'at the moment', so I don't think they're off the hook yet."

"We'd better get on with helping them solve the case then." Rohan rubbed his hands together. "So we have an explanation for Mervyn's rather dubious artwork. What did they say about his links, if any, to Josephine Hillson?"

"Oh, that was very sad." Esther thought back to the conversation she'd had earlier that day. "Remember that young man that was killed in the car crash? It was Sal

Wootton's husband, Mervyn's brother, Sean."

"Hang on," Rohan began to object, "that's not the name in the newspaper article we found."

"Yes, that threw me at first. Apparently Sean was a bit of an actor. He'd done a lot of local stuff and was about to play his first professional role. But there was already a member of Equity called Sean Wootton, so he took a different stage name."

"And that's the one the newspapers used?"

"Precisely. And that's why we didn't spot the link. The inquest was obviously done in his real name, but the newspaper's error wasn't picked up in time and that's the version that ended up in the archives."

"I'm confused." Olga wrinkled her brow. "If the police cleared Josephine of any blame, why would Veronica suggest that Mervyn might be responsible for her aunt's death?"

"According to Cath, there's been more contact between the two families in the past few months than there has been since the inquest. Apparently, Josephine found out Mervyn was working in Exeter and went to see him at work. It upset him quite a bit. He'd managed to put it out of his mind and there she was, dredging it all up again."

"Does he still blame her?"

"Cath says not. In fact, it was quite the opposite. Josephine felt guilty and wanted to make amends."

"And how was she going to do that?"

"Neither of them could offer any clues to that." Esther scratched her head. "It seems like she made some sort of offer to Mervyn but he wasn't interested and told her to sling her hook. And when Cath tried finding out what the offer had been, he wouldn't tell her. At least, that's what she assured me."

The three sat in silence, reviewing what they'd just heard. The ringing of a phone broke into the calm. Olga fished hers out of her pocket, while Rohan glanced down at his device lying on the table in front of him. Esther jumped up and ran round to the other side of the bar. "It's mine, I think." She grinned. "We really must change our ringtones so they're different."

Watching her face as she listened to the voice on the other end of the phone, Rohan saw the exact moment when her mood changed. He waited anxiously for her to disconnect the call.

"That was Sal. Cath's just had a call from the police station in Torquay. Mervyn Wootton walked in there a couple of hours ago and confessed to the murder of Josephine Hillson." Esther looked across at her two friends and Rohan could see the concern on her face. "The two women are distraught. They don't believe Mervyn did it. And after talking to them today, neither do I."

CHAPTER 35
THURSDAY 12ᵀᴴ SEPTEMBER

"Hello, yes, can I help you?" The voice on the entry phone was male, slightly hoarse and very, very cautious.

"Mr Foster? It's Rohan Banerjee. We spoke on the phone?"

"Oh, right." There was a pause. "You'd better come in then. Take the stairs down to the basement."

Rohan looked at Esther and raised his eyebrows. "That doesn't sound too welcoming. He was fine on the phone."

"Maybe that was because you took him by surprise. Now he's had time to think…"

There was a buzz and the lock clicked. Rohan pushed the door open. The hallway was large and painted in bright blues and greens, echoing the chessboard pattern of tiles on the floor. Carved wooden newel posts gave onto two staircases, one leading down to the basement and one up to the first floor. At the back of the hallway, a door stood open, giving access to a small garden area which seemed to be overflowing with shrubs and flowering plants.

"How beautiful." Esther walked to one of the newel posts and ran her fingers over the delicate carvings.

"Thank you. My son is very talented. He made them as a fiftieth birthday present for me." The voice made Rohan jump and, judging by Esther's little squeak of surprise, he wasn't the only one. Standing at the top of the upper staircase was a short stout woman with blonde curly hair. She was dressed in a flowing caftan and her sun-tanned feet were pushed into jewelled flip-flops. A pair of sunglasses could just be seen, peeping out from her curls. Long earrings swung and a collection of bracelets jangled as she walked down the stairs to meet them.

"I'm Arabella Prescott." She held out her hand. "Dylan's my son."

At that moment, footsteps were heard on the lower staircase. Dylan Foster was as dark as his mother was blonde, but shared her propensity for curls. His flowed down to his shoulders. It looked to Rohan as if Dylan took after his father, whoever that might be, since he didn't get his height from his mother either. Towering above her, Dylan went to stand next to Arabella. He smiled shyly at Rohan and Esther.

"Dylan told me you were coming, and I suggested I join you, if that's okay?" Arabella's tone made it quite clear to Rohan that she was going to be there whether he thought it was okay or not. "Let's sit in the garden, shall we?" She led the way around the side of the staircase and out of the back door.

Once outside, it was clear to Rohan that his original impression had been far from accurate. The garden was anything but small. But it was divided into a number of secluded areas, outdoor rooms really, each one overflowing with foliage. Arabella took them to a large central area, where a table was surrounded by six upright chairs. A huge umbrella provided shade for those who required it.

Arabella planted herself in the sunniest spot. "I understand you want to talk about Josephine Hillson?" She was obviously going to take a much greater part in this conversation than her son. "Dylan's already spoken to the police and answered their questions satisfactorily. Why do you want to talk to him?"

"I'm a private detective. I've been asked to look into the death of Miss Hillson."

"Asked by whom, may I enquire?"

"I'm afraid I can't divulge that, Ms Prescott." Rohan wondered about the different surnames, but decided that wasn't important at the moment. "My associate, Ms Steele, saw your son coming out of Miss Hillson's cottage a couple of weeks back. Josephine told her he was an old friend from way back. We wondered if he could give us any background that would help us." He bit his lip and tried to look pathetic. "To be honest, I'm a bit stumped at the moment."

"You know she tried to blackmail me…" It was the first thing Dylan had said so far and it sounded petulant. Arabella patted her son's arm.

"But you've talked to the police and cleared that up, Dylan, so it's not important."

"The thing is, Ms Prescott, in a case like this, you never know what's important and what isn't." Rohan turned to Dylan. "Can you tell me about the blackmail, Dylan?"

"She thought I'd done something terrible when I was a child." He paused and seemed to be struggling against breaking down. "In fact, so did I."

"Until I put him right, just yesterday." Arabella chewed on a lip. "I had no idea he'd been blaming himself all these years for his brother's death."

"And Miss Hillson tried to blackmail you?" Rohan was still trying to forge a connection with the son, rather than the mother.

Dylan nodded. "Yes. She was my companion for a while after my brother died and I used to have nightmares…"

Esther twitched one finger, her sign to Rohan that she had a question. He nodded at her.

"Was this during the time she took a break from teaching?"

Arabella nodded. "Yes. Hilly had a drinking problem." She paused and then appeared to come to a decision. "That's how we met." The words seemed to be being dragged out of her. "I was a heavy drinker from the early days of my marriage. Then after my other son, Dylan's brother, died, I decided I needed help and I went into rehab. Hilly had been there for a while and was much further down the road than I was. We got on so well, she became an unofficial sponsor. And for a period of time, she lived here with us. She was looking after Dylan and me at the same time."

"And was that when she had the car accident?"

"She came to us after the accident. She was already sober by that time, but the crash knocked her back both physically and mentally. I think working with us gave her time to heal. So the situation was mutually beneficial. She was with us for a couple of years and after she went back to teaching, we kept in touch."

"So it must have been a great shock to find out she was a blackmailer?"

"A terrible shock. Especially for Dylan." Arabella stared into the distance for a while and then shook her head. "In fact, I still find it hard to believe. She always struck me as so kind-hearted. And she would do absolutely anything for that niece of hers, absolutely anything. In fact she treated her more like a daughter. Comes of having no children of her own, I guess." She shook her head once more and sighed. "It just goes to show how wrong one can be."

CHAPTER 36
FRIDAY 13TH SEPTEMBER

"Whew, that was a lunch and a half, Olga. Thank you." Rohan threw himself back in his chair and rubbed his stomach.

"And not having to cook it myself makes it even better." Esther beamed from the other side of the table.

"You're both most welcome. You deserve it after all the shifts you guys have been putting in." Olga was delighted to have the opportunity to look after her two friends for a change. Although she did have an ulterior motive. But that could come later. "And, Esther, there's plenty left over for you to take back to the farm, so you won't have to cook for your father tonight either. And don't forget you can have a lie-in tomorrow as well. I had a word with Tommy, and he's going to get his own breakfast; and I'm helping Melanie in The Falls."

Having seen how tired Rohan and Esther were becoming, and realising they'd barely had any time off since Charlie, Annie and Suzy had left for Latin America, Olga had chatted to the Richardsons and other friends, and arranged for them to take over for a couple of days.

"Such luxury." Rohan stretched and yawned. "I may even take an afternoon nap later on."

Olga pointed down the slope to where comfortable loungers sat under the trees. "Help yourself. Or go for a swim, if you like."

"I'll take you up on that, even if Rohan doesn't. I brought my costume, just in case." Esther winked at their hostess.

"But before we all get distracted, I think we should just run through where we are with the investigation." Rohan sat up, blinking owlishly. Esther nodded and pulled her tablet out of her bag.

Olga hugged herself mentally. It looked as though her plan was working.

Rohan tapped his fingers on the table. "Okay, let's start with the Worcester twins. Anything more on them?"

Esther shook her head. "I had a chat with Caroline this morning. She seems to have calmed down a bit. And according to her, the boys are completely back to normal. They don't seem worried at all."

"Which may or may not be a good thing." Olga grinned and her two companions nodded their agreement.

"So what about young Dylan and his oh-so-very protective mother?" Esther had already brought Olga up to date on their meeting the previous day. "Any more thoughts on them?"

"We're a bit conflicted on that one, to tell you the truth." Rohan glanced at Esther who pursed her lips at him. "I can quite see young Dylan losing his temper in the heat of the moment and hurting someone."

"While I," Esther took up the story, "think he's far too delicate to do anything like that. While Arabella Prescott is so fiercely protective of her son, I could easily see her plotting a murder if her Dylan was being threatened."

"But she knew the threat wasn't real. So why would she need to protect him?"

"So she said. But we only have her word for Dougal's cause of death."

Olga could see this argument had been going on for a

while. "Well, that should be easy to find out, shouldn't it? There must be a death certificate somewhere."

"On my list to check out next." Esther made a note on the tablet.

"Ma'am, there are some ladies to see Miss Esther." Lindy had appeared so quietly at Olga's shoulder that she thought, not for the first time, of insisting her housekeeper wore tap shoes or wooden clogs rather than her normal crepe-soled sneakers. "They've been sent over from The Falls."

Olga looked across the room to see two women, one white, one black, standing shyly in the doorway. Before she could say anything, Esther jumped up and ran towards them.

"Cath, Sal, what are you doing here?" She grabbed their hands and pulled them into the room. "Olga, Rohan, this is Cath Wootton and her sister-in-law, Sal."

"We're ever so sorry to disturb you," Cath looked as if she wanted to curtsy to Olga, "but we asked in the pub, and they told us Esther was over here."

"We've had some news and we needed to talk to you," Sal said. "Correct some of the things we said yesterday."

Olga stood and smiled at the two women, trying to put them at their ease. "Sit down, ladies, please." She pulled out a couple of chairs for them. "Lindy, can we have some drinks? Tea or coffee?"

Once they were all seated once more, Esther smiled at the two newcomers. "Okay, who's going to start?"

"I will." It was Sal who spoke. "I had a call this morning from Josephine Hillson's solicitor. She's made me a major beneficiary in her will. Said the money was to make sure Sean's kids were able to put down deposits on their own homes." She choked up. "I knew she was planning something, but I had no idea what she was going to do."

"And how did you know?" Rohan put his head on one side and spoke softly.

"What? Oh, she contacted me a few weeks ago. Said she wanted to talk to me about making amends. I ignored her messages to start with, but she was quite insistent and finally, I decided to go and see her. I was there on the Sunday afternoon and evening that she died. I'd had lunch with a friend who lives near Coombesford and we went to the Summer Social together afterwards. But I never managed to get to talk to her."

"And Mervyn was there as well." Cath jumped in at that point. "He saw Sal in the distance. He told me last weekend." She leaned across and squeezed her sister-in-law's arm. "I'm sorry, Sal, I didn't tell you everything I knew before now."

"That's okay, Cath." Sal turned to Esther and Rohan. "Cath and Mervyn were suspicious of why I was there. We know he didn't kill Miss Hillson, but he thinks I did. And he's been very protective of me, ever since Sean was killed. That's why he's gone to the police; to confess."

CHAPTER 37

Once Cath and Sal had left for home, Rohan said he was going to stroll back to his lodgings at Steele Farm to pick up his swimming trunks. Olga lay back in her chair with her eyes closed, soaking in the late afternoon sun, while Esther got online and researched the UK archives for death certificates.

It didn't take long to find. "Here you go. Dougal Brian Foster. Died 19th August 2001. Cause of death, congenital heart failure." She pulled a face. "Okay, Rohan wins. Arabella Prescott knew Dylan had nothing to fear from a blackmailer or from the police. So we can cross her off the suspect list. He'll be delighted when I tell him that."

On a whim she also checked the birth certificates for Arabella's sons. Nothing unusual there. Dougal born thirty-two minutes before Dylan. Mother Arabella Foster née Prescott; Father Reginald Foster.

And then, remembering something Arabella had said in passing, Esther searched for Veronica Penfold. And drew a blank.

"That's odd."

"What?" Olga was instantly alert.

"Well, I can't find a birth certificate for Veronica Penfold."

"Was she ever married?"

"Not as far as I know. And she's registered as a voter at the same address as a Mrs Penfold, who is presumably her mother."

"Maybe she's adopted. Oh…" Olga's eyes widened, and she pointed excitedly at the keyboard. "Try Veronica Hillson."

Esther's fingers flew across the keyboard, and sure enough, there it was. Veronica Hillson. Mother Josephine Hillson, father unknown. Esther sat back in her chair, a slow smile spreading across her face. And she could read her own thoughts reflected in Olga's face.

"So the upright retired schoolteacher was not only a recovering alcoholic with a taste for blackmail on the side…" Esther began.

"…she had a child out of wedlock and gave her up for adoption to her own sister and brother-in-law," Olga finished her sentence.

"Well, you two have been busy. I should leave you alone more often." Rohan was standing in the doorway leading out onto the terrace. "That's quite a leap forward you've made." He paused. "I wonder if Veronica knows?"

"She must do, surely?" Olga said.

"You'd think so, yes. But if she did, they kept up the aunt/niece pretence very well."

"Well, there's one way of finding out." Esther closed her tablet and slid it into her bag. "I promised to pop in this afternoon to see how Veronica was getting on now she's been discharged from hospital. Let's go and talk to her." She bent to give Olga a hug. "Thanks for a wonderful lunch, Olga, and for arranging this little break for us. I feel completely refreshed. You must let me return the compliment as soon as we're done working at The Falls."

"Oh, you don't need to do that. Just come back here later for that swim, and let me know how your chat with Veronica goes."

The door to Josephine's cottage was propped open and when they knocked, a strained voice called them in. They found Veronica sitting in the sunny study at the back of the house. Her bare feet were propped up on a stool and her shoes lay discarded to one side of the room. They looked mismatched and abandoned lying there, and Esther was seized by an urge to straighten them up side by side.

Their owner looked pale and exhausted. Esther thought back over everything Veronica had gone through in the past couple of weeks and wasn't at all surprised to see the state she was in. Were they about to make it worse for her? Esther hoped not. She was beginning to wish she'd left this visit until the next day. Or come on her own.

Rohan pulled up a chair and assumed what Esther called his neutral face. The one he often used when he had bad news to impart. "How're you doing, Veronica?"

"Getting there, thank you." She gave a weak smile. "Or should I say, thanks to your lady friend here."

"Oh, I'm not his…" But Esther realised it wasn't important at that moment. "I'm just glad I was in time."

Veronica coughed roughly and reached out for the water bottle on the table next to her. It was empty.

Esther jumped up. "Let me get you some more water."

"That's kind of you. There's a full pack in the pantry. And bring some for yourselves as well."

As Esther left the room, she glanced again at Veronica's discarded shoes. What was it about them that didn't look right? She wished she could work it out. She shrugged and dismissed her concerns.

The pantry was under the stairs, accessed by a narrow wooden door. There was no window in there and it was pitch black. Stepping forward gingerly, Esther banged her head against the side of a shelf. Cursing softly, she felt around for a light switch and finally found an old-fashioned pull-switch hanging just inside the door.

A single light bulb without a shade hung from the low ceiling. The packs of water were on the top shelf. Esther pulled out a couple of bottles, then remembered Veronica had offered some to her and Rohan, and grabbed two more. As she did this, the pack became unstable and tipped over, crashing to the floor and spilling bottles all around her.

"Are you alright in there?" Rohan's voice came from the study.

"Yes, I'm fine. Just me being clumsy. Tell Veronica not to worry. There's nothing broken."

She crawled around on the floor, picking up the spare bottles and returning them to the shelf. As she grabbed the last one, she saw something flash in the corner of her eye. White, plastic. And as she realised what it was, everything began to fall into place. Pushing it into her pocket and collecting the bottles of water once more, she switched off the light, closed the pantry door and returned to the study.

CHAPTER 38

"Did you know Josephine was your mother, not your aunt?" Esther's opening words, once she'd dispensed the bottles of water and they'd all drunk deeply, rather took Rohan by surprise. As they'd been crossing the green towards the cottage, Esther had emphasised they needed to be gentle with the woman who'd not only lost a close relative but had also been attacked and nearly killed soon after. But something seemed to have changed Esther's mind.

"Yes, of course I knew. Although she never told me. How stupid did she think I was? Those sorts of things are easy to find out these days." Veronica took another drink of water. "But not at first, I didn't. For a long time, I thought I was a favourite niece. And we always got on really well, so it didn't really seem to matter whether I thought of her as my aunt or my mother."

Then Veronica seemed to remember where she was and who she was talking to. "But why are you asking? And more to the point, how did you know?"

"Like you, I guess." Rohan still had no idea where Esther was going with this. "I looked it up on the internet. I used the archive of birth certificates. I'm guessing you found out via the adoption agency."

Veronica nodded.

"So it must have hurt to find out she was leaving a lot of her money to someone else?"

"Not really, no. I've got a good job. My adoptive parents had no other children, so I'll be the sole beneficiary when my mother dies. I didn't need Josephine's money." She paused and rubbed the back of her hand across her forehead. "Although it might have been nice to have been consulted before she made another family rich."

"You know the Woottons, don't you, Veronica?" Rohan suddenly had an inkling of the thoughts in Esther's head. He found them hard to believe, but realised they were running out of ideas. "You've known them for a long time?"

"I've heard of them, yes. They were a major factor in my aunt's life at some point."

"And yours too, I think?" Esther's voice was deceptively quiet. "Were you in the car when it crashed, Veronica?"

The nod of her head was so slight, Rohan almost missed it. There'd been mention in the reports of a passenger, but unnamed.

"Veronica, were you driving at the time?"

"No, of course not. Why would you ask that?"

"Because Arabella Prescott said Josephine would do anything for you, absolutely anything. I wondered if she was willing to take your place behind the wheel of a crashed vehicle. Maybe because she was sober. And you weren't?"

"How did you know?" The question was barely a whisper.

"I didn't until now." Esther sat up and resumed her normal voice. "But I realised why your shoes look so mismatched. Because they are, aren't they? One of them is built up to compensate for a limp that you developed after the crash. And the damaged leg is your right one. The one that would have been extended on the brake pedal when you hit and killed Sean Wootton."

Rohan thought hard. They were uncovering more details about Josephine Hillson's past, and about that of Veronica Penfold, her niece (or daughter, he guessed he needed to call her now). But where did that take them with the murder investigations? He struggled for other loose ends to pull.

"How are the police getting on looking for your attacker, Veronica?" His change of tack seemed to catch her off guard.

"They've not been in touch for the past couple of days. So I don't think there's any news at present."

"Oh, I don't think they're going to find your attacker any time soon." Esther sounded particularly bitter at this point. "Because there was no attacker, was there, Veronica?" She turned to Rohan. "I wondered why I saw no-one leaving the cottage as I was arriving. But at the time, I was too busy saving a life. Or thinking I was."

"But, Esther, you told me she was tied to the steering wheel. You're not suggesting she did that herself, are you?"

"That's exactly what I'm suggesting." Esther put her hand in her pocket and pulled out the white plastic she'd found on the floor at the back of the pantry. An extra-long cable tie partially closed in a loop, with a long tail sticking up. "I'm betting if I slipped these on my wrists and pulled that tail with my teeth, I could do a pretty good imitation of someone who'd been tied up."

"But why?" Rohan stared at Veronica. "Why would you do that?"

"To put us – and the police – off the scent." Esther worked her way through the final few steps. "Just like she did when she told you about Mervyn; and when she gave the police the little green book. Were you in on the blackmailing as well? What happened? A falling-out among thieves? Is that why you killed her?"

Veronica shook her head. "No, I knew nothing about the blackmail. Not until after she was dead." She laughed harshly and then coughed. "I have to say that was a side to the old bird I didn't expect. And judging by the names and dates in that book, she'd been at it for a long time. Maybe ever since she returned to Coombesford after getting her teaching job back."

"But why?" Rohan realised he was starting to sound like a broken record. "Why did you kill her?"

"She was going soft on me in her old age. She felt really guilty about hiding the true cause of the crash. Letting Sean Wootton take the blame for his own death. Sooner or later, she was going to tell someone. Probably the Woottons as she was getting so pally with them. And I couldn't risk that, now could I?"

Veronica took another drink of water and then picked up her phone. "I suppose you'll want to hang around to make sure I do this right," she said, as she dialled 999. "Hello? Police please. I want to confess to a murder."

EPILOGUE

"Thank you so much for the call, DC Wellman. Yes, I'll tell them. Goodbye."

Caroline Worcester disconnected the phone and stood with her eyes closed, revelling in the deep feeling of relief washing over her. Her boys were off the hook, completely exonerated. The presence of their DNA at the crime scene had been fully explained to the police's satisfaction and they had been eliminated from the enquiries. And since Josephine Hillson's killer had confessed and intended to plead guilty, they probably wouldn't even be called as witnesses.

"Mum, was that the police?" The quiet voice from the landing above was Paul's. She could tell them apart, even if no-one else could. But she could see Peter standing in the background, looking equally concerned. She knew her sons weren't bad lads, either of them. And they'd been through a really stressful time.

She turned and opened her arms wide. The smile on her face was enough to tell them everything was going to be okay. There was a thunder of feet as the pair ran down the stairs and threw themselves at her. The three jumped around the open-plan lounge for a few minutes before collapsing into a giggling heap on the sofa.

Finally some kind of calm was restored. Caroline climbed to her feet and gazed down at the two teenagers in front of her. "First thing in the morning, I want you to go over to The Falls and thank Mr Banerjee and Ms Steele for their help."

"Yes, Mum."

"And take them some chocolates, or flowers. Flowers would be better. You should have enough money left in your birthday fund for that."

"Yes, Mum."

"And don't think that just because this is all over, that I've forgotten you lied to me about that plan to pinch the money from the Summer Social. You're still grounded until the end of the month."

Two pairs of eyes stared at her. Two mouths opened to protest. She stared back at them, trying hard to hide her grin, as identical looks of resignation appeared on their faces.

"Yes, Mum."

Rosemary Leafield rose from the pew where she'd been sitting in silent contemplation for the past hour. She heard a footstep at the back of the church. Turning, she saw her husband trying to quietly tiptoe away. When he realised he'd been spotted, he waved a hand apologetically.

"Didn't mean to disturb you. I'll leave you in peace."

They'd not spoken unless absolutely necessary since their row of two nights before.

Rosemary sighed. "Joel, don't go. We need to talk."

He shrugged and walked up the aisle to join her. He must know she'd never lose her temper here in church.

They sat down and stared at the stained-glass windows above them for a long time. Finally he turned towards her.

"Rosemary, I'm so sorry. I should never have asked you to lie for me."

"No, you shouldn't. Nor should you have lied to me." He opened his mouth to protest, but she laid a finger across his lips to silence him. "I know, Joel. I know all about your bit on the side." At least about this one, anyway. "She called me."

"Why would she do that?"

She felt an intense flash of irritation and disappointment. Why had she called? That was what he took from this conversation? "She thought you'd killed Josephine."

"But that's ridiculous."

"Of course it is. And that's what I told her. But the key thing is that she told me about the affair, Joel, and you didn't. Not even when you were asking me to alibi you to the police."

There was a long sullen silence. Then: "I suppose you want a divorce."

"Of course I want a divorce, Joel. I want you out of my life and that of our daughters as soon as possible." She sighed deeply and bit back her anger. "But that's not going to happen, is it? I'm a vicar. If I divorce, I can no longer operate in the church. And I will not let you take my career and my vocation away from me as well."

"So we're okay then?"

"Oh, Joel." She shook her head slowly, wondering just how simple he could be. "We are very far from okay. But for the sake of our family, and my position in the community, we're going to keep up the appearance of being okay."

He got up and left her sitting alone in the church. And Rosemary wondered just how much she was willing to accept before she did something human for once.

When they reassembled at the manor that evening, Rohan and Esther took the sofa, sitting close together while Olga sat in the armchair opposite, keen to catch up on all the news. "So do you have any idea why Josephine Hillson had turned to blackmail?"

"None at all." Rohan shook his head. "Maybe she was in financial difficulties. After all, she'd been out of a job for some time, and those rehabilitation places aren't cheap."

"Or maybe she saw herself as some kind of vigilante," Esther joined in, "dispensing justice in her own way to people who were getting away with it, whatever it might be."

"Of course, she could just have been addicted to the power and the thrill of a double life. Who knows." Rohan shrugged. "I doubt if we'll ever know."

"Still, at least you found her killer, so that's one mystery solved. You did it again, you clever things." Olga clapped her hands and beamed at her two friends. "And you did it without Charlie and Annie."

"But we had quite a bit of help, nevertheless," Esther said.

"From whom?" Olga was very proud of knowing the correct way to make 'who' the object of a sentence.

"From you of course, Olga." Rohan laughed at her surprised face. "In fact, we were thinking of making you an official member of the team. If you'd like it, that is."

"Do you hear that, Bertie?" Olga bent to stroke the little black and white dog at her feet and hide the sudden rush of emotion. "Olga's going to be a sleuth."

"To the Gang of Three." Esther jumped up and held out her drink to chink glasses with the other two. "But let's hope we're not called back into action too soon. At least not until Charlie and Annie get back to take over The Falls once again."

ENJOYED THIS BOOK?

Reviews and recommendations are very important to an author and help contribute to a book's success. If you have enjoyed *Silenced at the Summer Social* please recommend it to a friend, or better still, buy them a copy for their birthday or Christmas. And please consider posting a review on your preferred review site.

ACKNOWLEDGMENTS

I am once again very grateful for all the support provided by my friends in the thriving community of writers and readers, both in Devon and beyond.

In particular, my thanks go to Carol Amorosi who once again acted as my alpha reader; and to my wonderfully insightful beta readers who never fail to find the mistakes I've missed (or tried to hide).

Berni Stevens (bernistevenscoverdesign.com) is responsible, as always, for the beautiful cover and Otis Lea-Weston continues to develop the map of Coombesford. Julia Gibbs (@ProofreadJulia on Twitter) made sure the final text is as error-free as possible. My thanks go to all of them.

I owe a huge debt of gratitude to my sisters, Margaret Andow and Sheila Pearson, for their analytical reading skills and ongoing cheerleading.

Finally my thanks go, as always, to my husband Michael McCormick, my fiercest critic and strongest supporter, who never complains, no matter how many times he has to read the manuscript.

ABOUT THE AUTHOR

I was born and brought up in Birmingham. As a teenager, essays and poetry won me an overseas trip via a newspaper competition. Despite this, I took scientific and business qualifications and spent more than thirty years as a manufacturing consultant, business owner and technical writer before returning to creative writing in 2006. I have written short stories and poetry for competitions, gaining a few wins, several honourable mentions and some short-listing along the way. I am published in several anthologies.

Under the Chudleigh Phoenix Publications imprint, I have published six collections of short stories, including two co-authored with Sharon Cook. I also write non-fiction, including a series on business skills for writers and self-publishing.

My debut novel, *Gorgito's Ice Rink*, was runner-up in the 2015 Self-Published Book of the Year awards. These days, I write crime: the *Jones Sisters* thrillers; and cozy crime in the form of the *Coombesford Chronicles*.

I am a member of several writers' groups including the Crime Writers' Association; ALLi (The Alliance of Independent Authors); and Authors in a Pickle, which grew out of the Women in Publishing community.

You can find out more about me and my writing on my website, by clicking the QR code.

OTHER BOOKS BY ELIZABETH DUCIE

Coombesford Books
Murder at Mountjoy Manor
Villainy at the Village Store
Calamity at Coombesford Church
Coombesford Calendar volume I
Coombesford Calendar volume II
Coombesford Calendar volume III

The Jones Sisters series
Counterfeit!
Deception!
Corruption!
Retribution!

Other fiction
Gorgito's Ice Rink
Flashing on the Riviera
Parcels in the Rain and Other Writing

Co-written with Sharon Cook
Life is Not a Trifling Affair
Life is Not a Bed of Roses

Non-fiction
Sunshine and Sausages

The Author Business Foundations series
Part 1: Business Start-Up (ebook only)
Part 2: Finance Matters (ebook only)
Part 3: Improving Effectiveness (ebook only)
Parts 1-3 (print only)
Parts 1-3 Workbook (print only)
Part 4: Independent Publishing

Printed in Great Britain
by Amazon